ATOMIC
BOMBSHELL

Canada's complicity in the manufacture
of the first atomic bomb

With Love,
Sylvia

John T. Schmidt
Sylvia O'Callaghan-Brown

Published by:
John T. Schmidt
R. R. 1 Standard, Alberta, Canada, T0J 3G0

Distributed by:
John T. Schmidt
R. R. 1 Standard, Alberta, Canada, T0J 3G0
&
Bunker To Bunker Books
Calgary, Alberta, Canada.

Canadian Cataloguing in Publication Data

Schmidt, John, 1923 -
Atomic Bombshell

ISBN 1-894255-20-8

1. Atomic bomb - Fiction. I. Title.
PS8587.C4565A86   2002   C813'6.   C2002-910415-7
PR9199.4.S39A86 2002

Map
Back Cover Illustration — Cathy Chapin

Book Production by Northwest Printing, Calgary, Alberta, Canada.

Printed in Canada

Introduction

During the Second World War the United States Army had soldiers in many war zones around the world. Few Canadians (or Americans) heard much about the largest of these battle zones which covered an immense area of northwestern Canada, Alaska and the Alaska Archipelago. The reason so little was known about this big piece of real estate was that the American military subjected it to top security and tighter security than anywhere else in the world.

Ironically, outside of a brush-fire skirmish with Japanese invaders at Dutch Harbor in the 1,000-mile archipelago, fewer shots were fired there than anywhere else and few casualties occurred in this wilderness war zone.

In spite of the mayhem that was generated during the war, the Americans carried out three projects which, in the last days of the war, were crucial in defeating Germany and Japan. They were:

- The Alaska Highway, providing a staging route along which 10,000 American lend-lease planes flew into the Battle of Stalingrad for the Russians and thus broke the back of the German wehrmacht.

- The Canol Pipeline Project, which was piggybacked onto the Alaska Highway and was kept alive past its usefulness to cloak the super-secret Eldorado mine activities at Port Radium, Northwest Territories. It, in turn, provided the uranium oxide used in the manufacture of the first atomic bomb in history that was dropped on Japan to end the war.

- The Americans and Canadians built in two years a road which the Japanese had successfully prevented Canada from building for 40 years.

By its very nature, the Canol Project proved to be so enigmatic that no one person knew what was happening at any one time nor at various times could predict if and when it would ever be completed. For instance, Prairie farmers driving trucks knew nothing of a wildcatting effort to find more oil in the Mackenzie River watershed to carry through the Canol pipeline to an oil refinery in Whitehorse, Yukon. Bush pilots, who provided taxi service, never knew of the fierce internecine fights between the army and civilians in Washington over Canol Project overruns at a time when the Japanese armed forces were the chief enemies. Practically nobody knew of the U.S. Federal Bureau of Investigation's presence on the project.

The complexities and complications were so many that the head management contractor was useless as a source for writing a chronological historical non-fiction manuscript. The authors, therefore, had to invent a vehicle to tell the story. That vehicle was a young Canadian newspaper reporter, Oscar Grove, who was commissioned by the FBI to file periodic reports on the project which were passed along to opposition senators in Washington.

With a FBI expense account, the young reporter romps all over the huge — but flawed — project for three years. The usual love interest of a novel is supplied by Coleen, a young American secretary working for the U.S. architect-engineering firm on the project. She is interested in knowing what Oscar is doing for the FBI and she introduces spice to his romp and something even more interesting. She has a portentous omen about the project which she urges him to chase down.

Neither of them fully understands the horrific consequences of the omen which befuddles them until the U.S. Air Force drops the first atomic bomb on Hiroshima. Located where they are, they are practically sitting on the biggest scoop of Oscar's life, but he has no newspaper in which to tell his story. He cannot break his cover as an employee of the FBI.

The genesis of this story was 1963 at Lower Post, British Columbia, on the Alaska Highway at the Yukon border. An explanation of an event which happened there cannot be told in a way which would brook 2002 political correctness. But the event sent me on a 10-year investigative search of events which grew more engrossing every day. Out of it came a book, "This Was No Frigging Picnic," in 1992 to commemorate the 50th anniversary of the start of Alaska Highway construction. That book was sold out in 2001. That book never told the Canol Project story. That story ended up on the cutting room floor.

At this point I feel I have brought the reader to a threshold of understanding the significance of the Canol Project in Canadian history. My grasp of Canol's significance was brought about with the help of hundreds and hundreds of people all over North America, most of whom had worked on the project. Acknowledging their names would prove to be a task more daunting than building the project itself. I have outlived a large number anyway.

However, there are three persons to whom I must acknowledge for persuading me to press ahead with this novel.

When my boss, C.B. (Cully) Schmidt, former managing editor of the Kitchener-Waterloo Record, heard of the copy which ended up on the cutting room floor, he counselled: "It would be a shame to see the Canol story go unreported. You did a lot of legwork; you should bring it into the public domain."

The incentive to follow the advice of Schmidt arose when the Canadian Society for Civil Engineering and the American Society of Civil Engineers dedicated the Alaska Highway as the 16th International Historic Engineering Landmark. Commemoration plaques were unveiled in September 1997: at Dawson Creek, British Columbia; Fairbanks, Alaska; Edmonton, Alberta; and Whitehorse, Yukon.

Son Bill Schmidt, a Vancouver, British Columbia engineer, who helped pay for the plaques, lent encouragement for a book reporting to those inside and outside the profession how the work was performed under extreme weather conditions through swamps, bush, rivers, mountains, permafrost, mosquitoes and audited by Japanese armed forces.

In today's digitalized society, an oral history using taped stories containing slanguage, customs, historical events, geographic locations, history and politics of half a century ago has its pitfalls. The author was fortunate in avoiding some of the pitfalls brought about by the generation gap when Sylvia O'Callaghan-Brown offered to come aboard to provide a second pair of eyes to cope with a 30-year-old amorphous stash of copy. Her practised eye spotted ambiguities, euphemisms and lack of detailed explanations. These obscurities were purged with slave-driver thoroughness. Nothing was taken for granted. A paragraph-by-paragraph battle translated and edited the copy into today's realities.

John T. Schmidt
Standard, Alberta, 2002

I

At exactly 12.05 noon daily the staff at the T-Bone Restaurant in Picture Butte, Alberta, hustled into action for the arrival of a tall masterly whirlwind who burst through the front door and flung his cowboy hat at the rack. Pauline, all six feet and an eighth of a ton of her with an ass like a bumble bee, was waiting with open arms for an imperative semi-adulterous bear hug. "Oscar," she breathed, "what can I do for you today — 12-ounce T-bone rare?"

"Yes, but I don't want to compete with the flies for it."

"Oh, you big dumb smart-ass," and she pulled him tighter to her breasts which had never been encumbered with D-cup.

Oscar Grove chowed down the steak, burped, checked out Pauline's frolicsome bosom, and sauntered back to the Picture Butte Bugle newsroom to pick up his assignments from Peck Barnard, the cynical, ebullient, cigar-chomping, rum-swizzling editor.

His patronage ended abruptly one spring day when an ashen-faced Oscar was frog-marched into the T-Bone by two strangers. He had no smart-ass sallies that day. One stranger was a tall hombre wearing sunglasses and a hat brim over his right eye; the other nattily dressed bozo charged in behind and hovered over both of them. They had pushed past the Bugle receptionist into the newsroom, grabbed Oscar and took him across the street to the restaurant's back booth. They chased Pauline away with admiring extramarital glances after she delivered the coffee. The hombre shot out a hand and said: "Name is Hughie Melvin, FBI, Seattle. This here bozo is Senator Frank Jacobs. He chases down crime, too."

Oscar stuck out his ink-stained hand. "I am Oscar ..."

"Never mind that, Oscar. We know all about you. I have a dossier on you." Oscar turned a shade whiter. He slopped his coffee. "W-w-w-hat have I done?" he whispered, then characteristically ventured, "Cripes, a real live American senator in Picture Butte! But then he doesn't have a string tie like Senator Claghorn."

FBI agent Melvin ignored Oscar's feigned flippancy. "We know you are a fine investigative reporter. We have seen some of your freelance copy in the New York Herald Tribune. Jacobs and I are convinced there may be some hanky-panky on that U.S. Alaska Highway construction project you wrote about in your country, but more so on its ancillary Canol Project. The generals and construction bosses are keeping a lot of undercover skulduggery away from the people in Washington."

"The Canol Project? This is the first time I've heard of it. How does it tie into the Alaska Highway?" Oscar asked.

"We know less about it than you," answered Senator Jacobs. "However, we think reporters can go in and find out what goes on quicker than flat-footed FBI agents or Senate subcommittees. I can't find a damn word about it in the budget estimates. It's got top-secret billing.

"Rumors picked up by Cecil (The Bull) Pickett, a FBI agent in Washington, are that it's got something to do with oil drilling. He's in charge of a special file on this project. We think a big-spending general, Brehon B. Somervell, is heading the project and we have placed his file under Cecil (The Bull) also. We want you, Oscar, to revive your press credentials and report anything you can find out about either to Cecil (The Bull). You'll like him despite the fact he goes roaring around like a castrated bull. Everybody in the FBI knows how he opens an interview: 'Would you totally agree or totally disagree, somewhat agree or somewhat disagree with the following statement?'"

Agent Melvin wrote a $5,000 expense cheque "to start you off." Oscar was taken aback how fast it all happened. But he was alert enough to say "the FBI can't come into my country to ferret out Yankee criminals." This brought a table-banging response from Jacobs: "Mr. Grove, the FBI is a government agency charged with investigating crime among Americans anywhere in the world. Some of us senators figure the army has purloined the U.S. Treasury by spending money in Canada with no accountability."

Trying to atone for shooting first and asking questions later, Oscar asked: "Sir, how did you like the series of stories I sold to the New York Herald-Tribune on the 18th Engineering Regiment moving out of Vancouver, Washington, to 'invade' the Yukon to start building a 300-mile section of the Alaska Highway from Whitehorse to Beaver Creek on the Alaska border?"

"Well," replied Jacobs, "like a lot of other Americans, I had no idea where Whitehorse is. But you are a genius, kid, as you filled us in on your stories on why this 1,525-mile road is being built to protect Alaska, how it is being built in 300-mile sections rather than starting at both ends and working toward the centre. You actually knew some of the GIs in the 18th and wrote stories from their perspective. You had a world-wide scoop. You told me a story I never knew a damn thing about previously."

"Yep, it all came about because of a chance visit to my cousins in Vancouver, Washington, a few weeks after Pearl Harbor. They had pitched in to help the 18th man the installations on the Pacific beaches. I got to know all the scuttlebutt about the orders the 18th received before being sent to Canada. The mood of people on the front lines against the Japanese treachery at Pearl Harbor was savage. They were like cornered rats: that the American nation would some day return terror with terror. I have an ominous feeling in my gut that before this show is over something cataclysmic will happen to defeat the Japs."

At that point Peck Barnard walked in to find out who had kidnapped his star junior reporter. After introductions, Melvin said "this is the toughest case the FBI has on record. We need somebody like Oscar as he is competent and sharp. We have already taken steps to release him from your employment to send him north for us." After the ritual war against flies, they all sat down and tied into 12-ounce T-bones.

Oscar related how he had come back from Vancouver to the Bugle all excited about the new defence road. "But I think Peck thought I was feeding him a line of crap. He remained cynical until I produced a map and showed him what an immense area I was talking about."

"Yeh, and the kid was going on about some cosmic gut feeling he had that you Yanks were going to use some new system to zap the Jap," Peck admitted. "But then when I found out the newspapers in Canada had given no coverage about seven U.S. Army engineering units (four of which were Negro) building us a 1,525-mile defence highway, I changed my mind and sent him up there as I figured the story was bigger than us. While he was up there for two weeks, I got on Canadian Press's ass in Toronto and asked if they knew we were fighting Japan in the northern bush mile by mile. This caught their interest. When Oscar came back he got on his typewriter and wrote up 20 stories about those Americans going to fight on Canada's soil. When I fired off this series to Canadian Press I thought the story he dug up should get as much space as the Battle of Britain."

"What's Canadian Press?" interjected Jacobs.

"Oh, it's a news-gathering co-op organized by 100 daily papers in Canada to feed them national news — just like your Associated Press."

At this point, Peck's face got red with anger and he jabbed his finger into the tablecloth enunciating the words "those fatheads in CP at Toronto, the Hog Town of Canada, refused to move the stories on the goddam dismal pretext that nobody was interested in what was happening in the bush in British Columbia, the Yukon and Alaska." He choked on a mouthful of steak.

"So what did you do to get the stories published?" Jacobs asked Oscar.

"Went home cursing, swearing and fulminating louder than the boss. But my cousin, Sadie, was there and she came up with a remedy. She simply said if those bastards in Toronto don't want my copy, go round them like the Germans did at the Maginot Line in France. We worked all night sending letters to all Canadian dailies and 60 in the U.S. offering them the series CP turned down. This series sold to 35 papers. We added a few more stories and made $4,000 in freelance fees. This provided us with some champagne living."

"You were pretty upset with your Canadian Press," sympathized Jacobs.

"Yes, we thought we were vindicated when the New York paper paid us $50 an article. I, as a Canadian, had known very little about the North previously. You Americans knew even less and Eastern Canadians knew even less than that. I took pleasure in expanding their knowledge of this unknown land. Back at the office I became a victim of the economics of trying to run a newspaper in wartime and got the great move sideways to the business beat. This brings me to today when you showed up."

In a couple of days Oscar was on his way back to Whitehorse to find some of the friends he had made in the 18th Engineering Regiment. He had reached Whitehorse by travelling the 110 miles of cliff-hanging suspense through the mountains on the narrow-gauge rickety White Pass and Yukon Railway from Skagway, Alaska.

After pulling into town, he had no difficulty finding the room at the Pig's Ear Hotel which the FBI had reserved for him. He had no difficulty finding his friends. More to his elation, he found the GIs would rather spill their guts any time to a hotshot card-carrying reporter than to a G-man or senator.

More importantly, Oscar found a friend who offered to share her table with him in a crowded restaurant. She clung to his hand and introduced herself as "Coleen Patterson, with a thirst for Scotch in a town where liquor is rationed." Gallantly, Oscar introduced her to his cache in his hotel room. It was a platonic affair until one night she began chasing her Scotch with Advocat — and then started chasing him. She outran him. The chase ended when he had to make a trip up the road to the construction forces of the 18th as they left Whitehorse to do their share of the 300-mile section of the Alaska Highway to Fairbanks, Alaska.

When he reached the base camp Oscar was amazed at the rough terrain the GIs faced and was further astounded at the speed at which they were moving through it. He pulled out his notebook and did some philosophizing about the way they were carrying out the fight:

"The green recruits have traded a fear of uncertainty in the U.S. to a fear of the unknown in the Land of the Midnight Sun. Nobody was sure in either case whether the Japs would pack the same wallop against the mainland as they did in Hawaii. When they arrived at Whitehorse the 1,400 were more than three times the population of that village. Indians outnumbered the whites and they showed less interest in the uniforms than did the more numerous dogs. Running along the plank sidewalks and unnamed streets, the dogs accompanied the curious GIs to the Yukon River to gawp at the river boats still tied up in the winter ice."

Oscar's buddies were still standing in awe of the confusion in travel directives and counter-directives that brought them north. The only thing for sure was their determination not to leave the U.S. thirsty. That objective was pursued "so earnestly that 50 men per barrack missed bed-check the last three nights stateside."

When he finally met up with them, Oscar found the GIs in the 18th were not the bunch of devil-may-care, beer-swilling good fellows out on a lark who had first arrived at the job site north of Whitehorse. The Japanese had landed an army at Dutch Harbor in the Aleutian Islands. That had scared the pants off everyone.

In his first quick report to Cecil (The Bull) Pickett, Oscar said "men who had been beekeepers, ribbon clerks, fruit pickers, students, cowboys and mechanics had become relatively good truck drivers, heavy equipment operators and carpenters. When 50 pieces of heavy machinery arrived and had to be worked 24 hours daily, this required 175 operators the regiment didn't have. The problem was solved by taking men from the ranks and placing them with regular operators for a day or so. A few days later the pupil took on a pupil, I was told by Sgt. Speed Werkmeister of Denver."

"Hey, who's this Speed Werkmeister — everybody's favorite German uncle?" Cecil (The Bull) shot back.

"He's my favorite GI: a big grinning regular fellow with a nobby nose and a happy-go-lucky barrack-room lawyer who keeps us all laughing right to the last drink. He drives the brass a little crazy breaking regulations but he's always right — a self-starter who's out to win the war without rules."

Werkmeister was enthusiastic about the way the job was going. "At any time day or night this spirited troop could be seen defying military road-building regulations — and getting away with it. Had an experienced civil engineer taken a look at the terrain we faced, he would have said it was impossible to go through at the speed the army demanded. When all said and done, that's the way the Americans are winning the war: not so much by textbook military strategy but rather by fielding ingenious civilian volunteers who have thrown away the military manuals and disciplines," he told Oscar.

"For instance, it was against the rules to knock down trees with trucks. But when it was discovered trees up to six inches had such shallow rooting they could be easily knocked over, the truck drivers went through them rather than around them. It was the same in moving to a new location; the officers who went with the drivers to see regulations were carried out simply gave in when they saw a new system for moving convoys through muskeg. I lined up a dozen trucks to push the first one through, then that driver turned around and winched the rest through," Werkmeister concluded.

Werkmeister's method was hard on trucks but it worked. It even impressed Lieutenant "Red Death" Berry, he of the standing order: "Never stop once you get going; leapfrog over the obstacles and around each other."

"Berry was startled when our boys returned one day at noon from what was to be an all-day move through muskegs. He ran up to see what was up. What happened? Laconically I told him 'nothing'. Obviously he thought we had dumped our loads somewhere," Werkmeister told Oscar. "But old Captain W.T. Robbins, our taskmaster company commander, liked the ingenious method and told Berry to leave us alone."

Werkmeister took a liking to the keen young spark from Picture Butte who picked up on everything and asked all the right questions. From time to time he took Oscar along this preliminary road the GIs were smashing through the bush. Their work would allow civilian contractors to come in next summer to build a high-speed highway.

He was with Werkmeister at Mile 1020 where the bulldozers had ground to a dead stop and, some predicted, never to start again. But Werkmeister patiently explained "the obstacle is that no bridge has yet been built across the Slim's River at Burwash Landing. This was at a point where the road was to be taken across the river to proceed along the west side of Kluane Lake."

"So what's going to happen?" queried Oscar.

"Commander Robbins put in a call to send in the 73rd Light Ponton Engineering Regiment and its pontoon rafts to ferry the 18th's heavy machinery across Kluane Lake. You can see that 23-ton bulldozer on one of those rafts with Corporal Thaddeus O'Flasky in charge. This small raft is grossly overloaded, with only about two inches of freeboard. The launch, Josephine, is towing it," Werkmeister pointed out.

"How do you spell pontoons?" asked Oscar when Thaddeus reached the makeshift dock.

"The army preferred the French version, 'ponton', for the name of the regiments but used the anglicized word, 'pontoon', in reference to the type of rafts it uses. Not much sense, but true," Thaddeus explained.

"Where'd you get that lunker, the Josephine?" pursued Oscar.

"We rented her from Papa Jean Jacquot, a fur trader at Burwash Landing. She's leaky and her engine sputters and two crew work top speed bailing her out to keep her afloat. I was scared to death in the middle of the lake looking along the 100-foot tow rope to see my big bulldozer riding sideways atop the water, with two men in life jackets nursing the raft's motors. At mid-point a treacherous wind blew up a few waves and they grabbed axes to cut the lines if we sank. We didn't and now my bulldozer is being used to build the road across a formation of solid rock half a mile long rising at a severe angle from the water to 6,000 feet. About 400 feet above the water our experts found a toehold and powder monkeys are suspended from it to bore holes to enable the 18th to blast out a ledge for the road."

Oscar was the victim of the daily practical joke of the powder monkeys when he stayed overnight at the 18th's camp below the big rock. At the end of their night shift, the drillers took great delight in setting off a dynamite charge just before the bugle blew first call in the morning. He, along with all the GIs, was literally blown out of bed by the concussion. The GIs came tumbling out shouting dire imprecations at the culprits through sleep-blurred eyes. The powder monkeys were guffawing but were being cursed louder than the Japs.

Near the completion of this difficult blasting project, Oscar observed an unusual incident. Badly injured in a trucking accident, a private had to be airlifted to hospital in Whitehorse. To pick him up, a biplane on floats was despatched to Kluane Lake the next morning. That same morning the blasters had placed 30 cases of dynamite in the cliff face to make the last and largest blast. At the same moment that the chief pushed the handle, the Josephine rounded the point and was heading for the makeshift dock near the cliff. Despite the frantic efforts of the men to wave her off, the skipper didn't understand and kept on coming. And just as the charge went off, the mercy flight was making its landing approach on the lake.

"With a mighty roar that seemed to lift the whole mountain and shook the bones of every man, hundreds of tons of rock blew towards the lake. For a half mile rocks speared the water and stones showered the campsite. The Josephine was encircled by a landslide of boulders larger than herself — but inexplicably she was unscathed. The plane's serene approach was shattered by the concussion that buffeted it wildly about. Miraculously the plane escaped the hail of rocks that lifted up to meet it," Oscar marvelled.

Another spectacular event Oscar witnessed a few weeks later near the Kluane Lake rock was the official opening ceremony of the highway at Soldiers Summit.

Leading up to the ceremony, a bulldozer from the 18th met a bulldozer from the 97th Engineering Regiment, a Negro unit coming south from Fairbanks, at Beaver Creek. The meeting of the two signified the preliminary road had been punched through.

There were still some bridges to be built and upgrading to be done but both the government and military authorities of Canada and the U.S. decided to cut a ribbon and hoist a few glasses November 20, 1942.

On the appointed day, Oscar tried to take notes about the ceremony but his right hand shivered so uncontrollably in a wind chill factor of 50-below that he gave it up. "But I will always remember that front and centre were Alfunce Jalufka, a sheriff and farmer from Kennedy, Texas, representing the 18th, and Corporal Refines Sims of Philadelphia from the 97th, the bulldozer operators," he wrote Cecil (The Bull) Pickett in Washington later. "Sims and Jalufka may have been cold but not nearly so cold as the eight Royal Canadian Mounted Police constables who stood opposite them for what seemed like hours before the golden scissors were produced. The Mounties appeared at 10 a.m. wearing nothing over their famous crimson tunics. As their only concession to the cold they wore fur hats instead of the usual broad-brimmed frontier hats. Their dress crimsons and knee-high leather riding boots offered no protection for them. Most of the Americans had never seen the Mounties in their dress uniforms nor did they realize they were literally frozen to the spot standing there rigid and straight listening to all that quality bullshit.

"As soon as there was a slight pause in the speeches, the Mounties did a right turn as one man and marched with military precision back toward the tent. Only about half-way there they broke ranks and ran inside. Setting a record time for a quick change, they appeared in buffalo coats and mukkluks and marched smartly back again."

Colder even than the RCMP were members of the 18th's 25-piece band, the only regimental band on the project. Despite their best efforts, the cold defeated the "Star Spangled Banner" and the less-familiar "God Save the King." Back in the warm camp, however, the band played Viennese waltzes beautifully while huge roasts of moose were eaten, washed down with specially hoarded liquor.

Oscar rubbed shoulders with J. Frank Willis and Peter Stursberg who came in from the Canadian Broadcasting Corporation and fed an actuality broadcast to the Mutual Broadcasting System of the U.S. They were on a laughing jag about their microphones picking up a strange clicking sound when Health Minister Ian Mackenzie of Canada rose to speak.

"There were some frantic moments until Frank found the source," said Stursberg. "It was the sound of a shivering minister's false teeth clicking into a mike. He had given into the blandishments of a parliamentary assistant to doff his coonskin coat for a photo opportunity. He was colder than anyone on the scene."

Oscar fed the CBC duo with another human interest story that day. The top U.S. military man, General J.A. O'Connor, had hit the sack early after the party. He had no sooner drifted off to sleep than a GI from the 97th with a bit too much rum under his belt shook him awake.

"General," he said, "will you autograph my program?"

General O'Connor pushed back the flap of his eiderdown and blinked several times. Privates do not wake generals to make frivolous requests whether drunk or sober.

"What'd you say, private?" he barked.

The Negro lad saluted and repeated his request and, much to his own surprise, O'Connor heard himself saying "yes."

While the now-frightened dogface waited, the officer sprang out of the sack in his longjohns and, putting on his spectacles and finding his pen, signed the all-important program of a great event not only for the United States but Canada.

There was one Soldiers Summit incident Oscar did not feed to the CBC newsmen as they were not around next day. To put a new scare into the Japanese, the U.S. Army sent off a convoy of munitions-laden trucks towards Fairbanks as part of the Soldiers Summit ceremony. Oscar recognized one of the drivers as an old friend, Larry Pedee of Toledo, Ohio. Pedee grabbed him next day after breakfast and, with a conspiratorial command, he said "come with me. I've got something to show you."

With a querulous furrowed brow he jumped into a vehicle with Larry. They drove a couple of miles up the road and around a bend out of sight were those same trucks that had been at Soldiers Summit.

"Holy shit, what goes on?" Oscar bellowed.

"Shh. This is a super-secret. The bridge over the White River has not yet been completed. Also there are seven bulldozers still stuck in the ice in the river. This accident happened because some members of the 97th came roaring down the road in a truck to attend the opening ceremony and went through the ice in the shallow crossing. They had to use seven bulldozers to rescue them, but the bulldozers got stuck too. So we had to park the convoy here until they get the mess cleaned up."

"My God, what a ball the CBC would have had if they'd have got onto this story," Oscar whispered. Then he grinned and said to Larry, "well what have you got to say?"

"Thank you for asking me, my friend. In my most stentorian voice I'd like to tell the world this. For Canada, the Alaska Highway is a long-delayed trade route which has been awaited for decades. For the United States, this highway gave its army a new route to expedite strategic weapons to the Russians for attacking the German now-exposed underbelly. These loads will see Japan's worst fears materialize in a few weeks. God save the King. God save the President."

"This deserves a drink," said Oscar and he pulled out a mickey of overproof rum. That day he managed to hitch a ride back to Whitehorse over the new unfinished road to see Coleen and get a report off to Cecil (The Bull) Pickett.

There was too little activity for Oscar to send daily reports to the FBI. On slow days he spent time in the officers' mess reading about the war in outside papers and magazines and listening to local gossip. A few days before Christmas he heard a rumor that new orders had been cut for the 18th to pull out of the Yukon to build an airport runway at Shemya in the Aleutian Islands.

A week later somebody came in and shouted "they're here!" and the mess cleared out into 50-below weather to welcome a frozen regiment of GIs back to "civilization." They had spent 36 hours riding open dump trucks, the only transportation available.

Oscar found Werkmeister, Larry Pedee and some of his friends in a three-block line-up at the public bathhouse. Before they cleaned up, he spirited Werkmeister and Larry away to a bar to achieve their priority objective after nine months in the bush of a couple of barely remembered Canadian Club rye and gingers. The FBI expense account took a beating that night. Then came the second objective of a hot bath to free them from grime-covered underwear, plus a couple of more drinks to loosen the lips of Werkmeister. He was livid with rage:

"I was given the unenviable task of transporting the regiment back to Whitehorse in a 240-mile 36-hour death march on wheels at an average of six miles an hour," he winced and hovered over the heat, and continued his indictment against "those bastards in the U.S. War Department who got us onto this fucking project but didn't make any plans to transport us off the project at 50-below.

"Word of American prisoners prodded by Japanese bayonets on jungle death marches had reached us and we were appalled. But those buddies of mine forced to ride in the only available transportation, 70 open dump trucks, suffered as much. Had the Japanese carried out such a march on the Alaska Highway, they would have perished first. We hadn't gone 10 miles when we knew we were involved in a terrible ordeal of frozen legs. We lost 41 trucks from frozen fuel lines in that frigid operation. That ordeal made soldiers of us all."

Later, when he had had a bath and donned a clean uniform, Werkmeister confided "that order to move us out was cut none too soon. By the time it came, the 18th was operating with equipment that was practically junk.

"We had a hard time getting repair parts and had run our fleet 'into the ground.' Nearing the end, if a six-cylinder vehicle ran on five sparkplugs with a connecting rod removed, the driver thought it was a good truck. He would even be satisfied if the vehicle ran on four! 'Shorty' Curly, our blacksmith, who was built like a gorilla, was a genius at fashioning parts the bureaucrats failed to deliver. What he couldn't make, the drivers cannibalized from out-of-order vehicles. The practice was so prevalent our orders were not to leave a vehicle even if a driver had to stay with it all night and guard it with his life. Leaving a truck was a signal for another company's mechanics to raid it for the left rear axle as, for some reason, it was always the left ones that broke."

"I have picked up some hysterical yarns about parts that disappeared while drivers were having lunch," said Oscar.

"Without a word of a lie, I can tell you we laughed for three weeks about a Canadian trucker who ran out one cold morning and jumped into his truck after an overnight stop. He started the motor and when he put it into gear it didn't move. He jumped down and found thieves had stolen the entire rear end of the truck and left it up on the blocks. He cooled his heels two weeks waiting for a new rear end," laughed Speed.

Oscar was unable to assist in the third objective of his buddies: namely, women. But at a wild party at the Whitehorse airport hangars, an anonymous poet described their plight:

> *Somewhere in the Yukon where*
> *The nights were made for love;*
> *Where the moon is like a searchlight*
> *And the northern lights above*
> *Sparkle like a diamond necklace in*
> *The silent and calm of night:*
> *It's a shameless waste of beauty*
> *When there's not a girl in sight!*

All good things must come to an end and for Oscar it was the 18th's departure into another unknown project at Shemya. "I'm not sure I'd like to be in your shoes," he confided to Speed.

"Before we leave tomorrow, I want to show you something," Speed reassured him. "I want you to take a look at the esprit de corps our regiment has developed. We have survived one of the most extravagantly praised and loudly damned ventures in modern military history. We have built more miles of road than any of the other six regiments. We have become hardened soldiers no longer wet behind the ears. We have collectively been told the road is a miracle of engineering skill, but we think this is puffery and crap."

And then Fred Rust, the regiment historian who had been listening acquiescently, spoke up with another speech which Oscar memorized:

"The project was not a miracle. No great engineering skill was needed for its accomplishment. The highest individual credit should go to the top: Gen. W.M. Hoge, the first commander of the project, a true professional and an ultimate army officer. Although he wasn't there to see the project completed, he got it well under way. One of his greatest tributes was the understanding way in which he dealt with his subordinates. He permitted us to do our own work in our own way. This is the finest compliment a general can pay to his troops. We knew our friend, Hoge, had left the project in August. Later we were much distressed to learn he was transferred overseas on the recommendation of a senior officer who disliked his highway-building methods. But this is the way the army operates."

"I'll always remember what you have said about good leadership," commented Oscar.

Speed had the last word: "One of the top secrets was that the time of completion of the pilot road had been scheduled by the army for the end of two construction seasons. Then the project was to be turned over to the U.S. Public Roads Administration in 1944. But the speed at which our seven regiments worked surprised one and all. As you know, the PRA is the U.S. government agency which builds roads in the national parks. This pilot road has now been turned over to the PRA a year early and PRA is proceeding to let out contracts to civilian contractors to upgrade the pilot road."

On his way to the train next day Speed sidled up to Oscar: "What in hell are those pressure vessels we saw along the railway tracks? Are they going to start building submarines here?"

"Oh, God, Speed, don't make me answer that," pleaded Oscar. "It's highly classified and I know the answer but I'd end up before a firing squad if I told you. I'll write you after the war."

With that enigmatic remark, Oscar ambled off to dig into another big rumor that was titillating the boys in the pubs around town, also.

II

After the 18th pulled out of Whitehorse, Oscar was still in a state of ecstasy — like that of stealing a first kiss. He couldn't tell Speed Werkmeister he had a scoop under his belt. But one important detail was lacking. He had overheard a conversation in the bar that the pressure vessels Speed had espied were key parts for an oil refinery General Brehon B. Somervell, chief of the U.S. Army supply section, was bringing in from Corpus Christi, Texas.

Oscar had felt the tension among the U.S. military when they began to fear the Japanese Navy would interrupt supplies of aviation fuel from California refineries destined for Alaska Highway construction for the defence of the Northwest. Had the Japanese Navy been successful in knocking out the fuel supplies from California, it would have made redundant the 1,525-mile highway the regiments had succeeded in completing. General Somervell planned to bring in the oil refinery to foil the Japanese Navy.

"Yeah, that all sounds fine," Oscar confided in his ever-handy notebook. "But where in hell is Somervell going to find crude oil to feed a refinery when the nearest oilfield is 1,500 miles away?"

Had he been able to revert to his previous occupation, Oscar would have achieved the dream of every reporter: to get a national scoop, then he could be the centre of attention. He envisioned this scoop being carried on the front pages in Tokyo and demoralizing Japanese readers.

But he couldn't divulge the scoop. The FBI had sworn him to silence, dammit.

The puzzle of where the oil would come from kept him guessing, biting his nails and cadging double rums from big spenders in the palatial officers' mess. Then one night a latrine-o-gram rumor went the rounds and electrified the mess. The latrine was the best source of rumors and, while Oscar was on the can with a Reader's Digest, he heard two lieutenants breathlessly talking in riddles about "Somervell's going to tap

Norman Wells." Oscar tip-toed out and found a National Geographic map. Like most Canadians, he had never heard of Norman Wells before. How could Somervell, an American, know so much about the Canadian North? It stretched his credibility. Nothing he had ever read in fiction could prepare him for what the virile and decisive Somervell did.

Among the 1,000 orders he cut one day Somervell simply ordered a 625-mile pipeline to cut across the Mackenzie Mountains to tap into a small oilfield developed by Imperial Oil Limited at Norman Wells on the Mackenzie River. And, voila, the Canol Project came into being with an oil refinery dismantled at Corpus Christi and transported to Whitehorse.

When he first heard the whispers about the enormity of the project and the chutzpah of the man who conceived it, he couldn't get anyone inside or outside the U.S. Army to talk about it or confirm the rumor.

"Somebody must be pulling my leg," Oscar mused. "I gotta contact Cecil (The Bull) Pickett, the big wheel on the FBI's 'Somervell Desk' in Washington and report this." He was almost apologetic when the 'Somervell Desk' came on the blower. That desk was set up specially to keep track of the "top secret" projects by one of the biggest spenders in the world. Somervell shocked the Roosevelt Administration with his profligate billions, not telling them where they were being spent.

Cecil (The Bull) regarded him suspiciously: "You sure you haven't been into some of that 151-overproof rum? If this is true, Somervell has gone too far this time. Why, the cost of this Canol Project, as you call it, will be more than the Alaska Highway it is supposed to serve. Let me pull Somervell's file and see if he has ever been in any loony bins and I'll get back to you."

"Let me quote you what Robert Service said in his poem, The Cremation of Sam McGee: 'There's strange things done in the midnight sun'," Oscar reminded Cecil (The Bull).

When Cecil (The Bull) got back to him a couple of days later with the news that Oscar's rumor had proven true, he was awestruck. "They trained that bastard to spend money. Nobody here knows how much he well spend on this project but we want you to find out. Not even President Roosevelt knows."

Oscar felt instinctively something was wrong with the Canol Project after observing Cecil (The Bull)'s rancor with Somervell. His audacious ability to "mine" Uncle Sam's Treasury was devious. He was determined to find out if Somervell knew where the bodies in the Roosevelt Administration were buried.

Armed with 25 questions about Somervell, Oscar returned to the officers' mess. He hit pay dirt when he stumbled on a Somervell biography in the reading room. The bio took his breath away.

"I was converted to an instant fan from a critic," he wrote in his notebook. "He's one of the greatest military strategists since Attila the Hun. He's as great a statesman as William Pitt! He had previously become an organizing genius in the service of his own government."

The bio showed Somervell had been seconded by the U.S. Army to the Roosevelt Works Progress Administration to supervise the government's job-creation initiatives in New York City during the "dirty '30s." He had a budget of $10 million a month to keep 200,000 unemployed on projects ranging from archery contests to the construction of the $40 million LaGuardia Airport.

In a contretemps with some U.S. senators, Somervell was quoted: "My men in the front lines will receive the most and best materials available — and you will pay for them."

Oscar imagined Somervell took great pride in setting the Canol Project in motion and was very short with skinflint senators who alleged he was trying to militarize the U.S. economy: "I'll be glad to hand any senate critic a bayonet and tell him to go trade places with any GI in the field."

Even though he was now a fan of the great Somervell, Oscar prophesied to Cecil (The Bull) that the general was "sure to create animosity among civilians. He has no time for fools — even those with the moneybags. His chief aim in life is to beat the Japanese. He needs no surveillance from the FBI.

"Somervell's only blind spot is that he doesn't understand the vast distances in the Yukon and Northwest Territories. He thinks Canol is a straightforward project; that it's a very simple matter to land pipe, pumps and personnel in Whitehorse then build the west end of the pipeline through the scrub bush 325 miles to meet crews coming from Norman Wells. Holy cow, that 325 miles is the distance from Montreal to Toronto. But he has only geological survey maps which are sketchy and don't give him any idea of what he will encounter moving pipe into Norman Wells and through unknown mountains to meet the pipeliners from Whitehorse. I, myself, don't know a blessed thing about the route to Norman Wells. But I'm going to find out next week."

That trip "next week" proved to be a shocking disillusionment for Oscar. The three days the FBI allowed him for the junket turned into three weeks — but it was a learning experience. First, there was no way of going the 625 miles directly from Whitehorse to Norman Wells. Second, he couldn't get a reservation to fly Yukon Southern Airways for a week and a half to reach Edmonton, as the U.S. Army had priority.

The only alternative was to backtrack via the White Pass and Yukon Railway to Skagway, Alaska, to Vancouver by boat, then to Waterways via Edmonton by train and a Northern Alberta Railways branch line, hence by sternwheeler boat across Great Slave Lake and down the Mackenzie River to Norman Wells.

"Whew, a trip of 3,000 miles to travel 625 miles direct. What kind of a country is this?" he sighed to the White Pass station agent in Whitehorse. "I guess I'll wait for a plane seat. In the meantime there's nothing else to do but stay in Whitehorse and turn myself into an instant Northerner."

"Yes, I'm sure you will like walking around a town short of houses and booze but full of characters," sympathized the station agent. "You will see the smallest houses in Canada here because a shack is easier to heat at 40-below than a palace. If you hear shotguns going off in the night that's because people are scaring away woodpile thieves. The classical story is about the boys at the Bank of Commerce who were so desperate for wood they bought a huge pile of 12-foot hydro poles from the army then cut them up for firewood."

House size showed no favorites. General Patsy O'Connor, head man for the U.S. Army in Whitehorse, "inherited" a tiny house on the Yukon River waterfront built for the captain of one of the riverboats. It had a stone fireplace where he entertained Oscar and other guests with hot rums which he made with a blowtorch and soldering iron.

He'd spend a whole evening not exchanging a dozen words then tumble into bed in the master bedroom which was so small he had to climb over the footboard.

"G.A. Jeckell at the liquor store is my best friend," O'Connor joked. "He told me the reason he stocked overproof rum was there was no point in importing water into the Yukon!"

"How come (as a war measure) the rest of the provinces cut all spirits to 30 underproof and Jeckell still retails that overproof dynamite?" Oscar asked.

"Oh, they forgot to invite Jeckell to the conference where the decision was made. So he kept on retailing overproof."

At the Regina Hotel, Oscar found Americans had difficulty handling the overproof but, he was told by Bobbie Hill, a construction stiff from Missoula, Montana, "they never lost their respect for it. Like the time a gang of 50 from Minnesota came into our camp after an open-truck ride almost paralyzed them with cold. One asked for a drink and my buddy, Les Stone, came up with a bottle of this overproof. The guy seized it and took a couple of swigs. It almost took his breath away. His face turned red. His eyes bulged and he ran for the possum-bellied stove, pushed back the sliding door and spit a mouthful into the flames. Whereupon the red-hot stove spat a blue flame back at him. He screamed 'what the hell are you guys feeding me?' We laughed ourselves silly and showed him how to cut that overproof with water."

When the laughter in the bar died down, Jack Moore, a pipeline welder from Alberta sitting next to Oscar, swore up and down that demon rum was responsible for one of the best folk tales in the Yukon. The scene was set in the Whitehorse Inn. It was owned by Tee Cee Richards and managed by his wife, June.

"You-all know both were flamboyant characters who had a stormy marriage," said Jack as he pulled out a cigar. "Their most memorable row occurred at Christmas when June invited a lonely construction crew in for dinner. Twenty of them sat down to a table beautifully set with candles and her fine silverware. Tee Cee had cooked a 23-pound turkey in his bakery oven.

June, wearing a $300 gown she had brought in from Outside, knew how to preside over a fabulous spread like this. She had personally escorted all the guests to their seats. All were eagerly awaiting the appearance of their host with his carving knife."

Having set the scene and taking a big pull on his Torero cigar, Jack described his friend, Tee Cee, as "a big friendly bugger, with a good command of invective. But he was roaring drunk when he came into the dining room. After he'd had a chance to look over the guests, some of whom he didn't know, June asked him to do the honors.

"At that point the following exchange took place: 'All you well-fed bastards, you've come here to steal my silverware,' Tee Cee yelled thickly, glowering darkly at the guests. 'Tee Cee, you shouldn't talk to our guests this way,' June admonished. 'You're here to steal, too,' he shouted and, picking up the bird, he flung it the length of the table and hit her square in the chest.

"When it became evident the fight would not end soon, most of the guests got up and sadly left with their mouths still watering."

"Whatever happened to Tee Cee and his wife?" asked Oscar.

"Who knows?"

"And the turkey?"

"Maybe we'll never know," said Jack gulping another swig of rum.

Oscar was still chortling about the assortment of uproarious and outrageous characters he met in Whitehorse as he boarded a plane for Edmonton. The more he travelled the more he realized the isolation and nature of the Yukon did strange things to men's minds and souls. Some were in the Yukon of their own free will, fascinated by the mystique of the wild. Others were on the lam from the law or the draft. The slower pace of life in the Yukon brought out a swashbuckling sense of creativeness which drew plaudits from Outsiders. George Cameron Ford (Dal) Dalzeil, a bush pilot from Watson Lake, was one of those who saw the big scene.

When the plane took off from that airport, Oscar found himself sitting next to a bush pilot from Rochester, Alberta, Joe Irwin, who told him how Dalzeil became a legend in his own time by starting a taxi service for road construction personnel in an area where there were no highways.

Dalzeil came North to trap out of Dease Lake, British Columbia. In his early days he learned to live off the country with only a handful of shells in his pocket.

"He soon realized the country was too big for him to make a fortune unless he bought an airplane and learned to fly it. He took to flying like a bird but he gave his instructors apoplexy because of lack of discipline and flouting the rules," said Joe.

"Most bush pilots were expected to be communications links between the locals and the 'outside.' It was their duty to trade gossip and news. But not Dalzeil. He was a loner, not quite anti-social but a silent, close-mouthed type. He'd disappear and sleep rather than join prospectors, trappers, construction stiffs and other pilots gathered for a few drinks at night. But much gossip dwelled on him and his solitary ways and adventures."

"But he was a top-rated pilot?" pursued Oscar.

"Yes, sir, but his luck ran out in 1941 when Roy Gibson, commissioner of the Northwest Territories, was instrumental in having his pilot's license lifted for infractions of the game laws. However, he got it back in the most unexpected way. He received assistance from Cy Becker and Matt Berry, a couple of his old flying buddies, who were in Portage la Prairie running one of the Commonwealth Air Training Plan elementary flying training schools. They agreed to sign him up as a recruit but stipulated he had to write the RCAF exams. Gibson didn't think Dal would submit to this indignity as he had forgotten more about flying than any of the instructors knew. However, he did, passed with honors and was issued a new license." He was seconded by the RCAF to the wartime taxi service in the North, which became known as the Canol Air Force.

As Joe Irwin's last Dalzeil "story" ended, the Barkley Grow on floats splashed down on the waters of Charlie Lake to deplane passengers for Fort St. John, British Columbia (the plane had been on skis to make the landing on the frozen lake a month before). When Irwin got off, a friendly graying man across the aisle tapped Oscar on the shoulder, gave him a grin and introduced himself as Norman Stanton of Vancouver, a surveyor for the Canada Department of Transport.

"I heard my friend, Irwin, giving you a dry-cleaned version of Dal's biography. You might think this is a primitive air service; and I know the Yanks do also. But had it not been for Dal and other top bush pilots, us DOT people in the field and the Canada-U.S. Permanent Joint Board on Defence couldn't have accomplished as much as we have up to this year. I can't tell you how elated I am as a Canadian to finally see — after being stymied for 40 years — a highway from Dawson Creek, B.C. to Fairbanks, Alaska, being surveyed by the U.S. Public Roads Administration and being built by the U.S. Army (albeit as a military defence road).

"This Alaska Highway is not only connecting our Northern airports but the U.S. is upgrading these airports to all-weather status. God, this makes me feel as if we are going to make something of the Canadian North after all."

Oscar looked a bit puzzled: "I didn't understand your statement about the 40-year delay. I heard in 1938 the British Columbia government was trying to get some action in the U.S. for a road but nothing happened."

"Well, I'll give you my version of why Canada failed to build anything but a couple of winter roads in the Dawson Creek, Fort St. John and Fort Nelson areas. It was Japanese opposition dating back to 1900. This is a fact few Canadians realize about Northern development. You can check that out some time in the library at Picture Butte," said Norman with a grin on his face.

"Although there was not much road-building, Canada and the U.S. have been working 'underground' upgrading airports. Even so, we were not anywhere near as advanced as the Russians, who had cities of 100,000 in Siberia. We knew it could be done."

"How could this be?" interjected Oscar. "I never heard a word about this in the papers or in history courses."

"The Japanese regarded these upgrading activities as covert acts of hostility and persistently used diplomatic channels in attempts to have these improvements in Canada cancelled."

"Wha-a-a-t? This sounds crazy!"

"You must realize at that time Canada was still a colony of Great Britain and therefore the Japanese complaints were sent to the British Foreign Office. The beleaguered foreign office, harried with thousands of decisions, didn't wish to create a new enemy and it was easier to grant the Japanese requests and signal the Canadian government to restrain its northern development to shut up the Japanese."

"That sounds like the parent who receives a complaint about a brat and his only answer is 'sorry, but I can't do a damned thing with that kid,'" said the indignant Oscar. But there was more to come from Norman that helped to smooth a rough flight.

"The historians trying to fathom this Japanese diplomatic activity have always found the answer elusive. But they do agree that the Japanese psyche had an aberrant fear of being subject to military encirclement by, first, the Soviet Union, to which Japan had lost territory in a war at the turn of the century. The hated secretive Soviets were developing their North and this scared the Japanese. Secondly, the U.S., having purchased Alaska and the Alaska Archipelago from Russia in 1867 for $7 million, was slow to develop Alaska and Japan wanted it that way. Third, Canada, although a colony of Great Britain, was seen by the Japanese to be in league with Alaska to help develop the Yukon to build roads, railways and airports.

"The great empty North of both Canada and Alaska was the playground of a 'squadron' of quietly aggressive, devil-may-care bush pilots. They proved the airplane could shrink distances in the North. In the three years leading up to the war the bush pilots had worked surreptitiously with the DOT and the U.S. Federal Aviation Administration at airport improvements. When Canada entered the war with Germany the Canada-U.S. Permanent Joint Board on Defence was set up. This board called for further improvements and recommended to both Ottawa and Washington that the Japanese protests be ignored."

Now Oscar was beginning to see the picture. Canada had a big contribution to make to the U.S. war effort with its small airports that allowed the U.S. to set up its Northwest Staging Route for the defence of Alaska and the Aleutian Archipelago which stretched 1,000 miles from Cold Bay on the Alaska Peninsula to Attu Island near Russia's Kamchatka Peninsula. Dutch Harbor was the main military base.

At this point Norman fell silent and Edmonton came in sight. He looked obliquely at Oscar and said, "I hope you appreciate my little history lesson."

"Yes, and you have got me riled up enough to send a thank-you note to Hirohito for allowing us to have the Alaska Highway he has denied us for so long! I reiterate, it's marvellous that we, with help from the Yanks, are going to complete in two years a road they stonewalled for 40 years. Historians are going to regard this as one of the world's greatest engineering landmarks," said Oscar as they prepared to disembark.

"I agree with you 98%," replied Norman. "The one downside is the Yankee penchant for fighting not only against the Japs, but among themselves and with their friends and allies as well."

"Are they trying to step on us?"

"Well, the military is. Our DOT and their military have differing terms of reference. The DOT is upgrading a string of civilian airports to the posh standards and enduring design of those in the U.S. After the war these airports will be used to give Canada access to Russia and the Orient.

"On the other hand, the U.S. is in here building airports on a temporary footing. All they're interested in is fast-tracking airports on a slap-dash basis to serve their needs for two or three months or three years, then withdrawing. Their needs are to drive the Japanese off the Pacific and flying lend-lease planes over the Northwest Staging Route in the back door of Russia to oust the Germans from Stalingrad."

"I guess the American military is being driven crazy by the measured pace of the middle-aged union men who work to rule, forgetting there is a war on," said Oscar ruefully.

"Well, no more than the DOT is being driven to distraction by these young bucks from Stateside who will work seven days a week without overtime. Old guys have no use for young guys who do shoddy work. The Americans also want to build a string of emergency landing strips to help pilots from the numerous crashes. And they want better air navigation systems built immediately."

Casting another sidewise glance at Oscar, Norman concluded: "You can see a political tug-of-war within a serious war is developing. I'm afraid the Canadians will have to give in to the U.S. gigantic war machine eventually."

Oscar was sure the FBI would be interested in the internecine aspects of Uncle Sam's "invasion" forces as nobody in Washington wanted to see a cold war break out with Canada before the Japanese were licked.

When Oscar alit from a cab at the Greenbriar Hotel in Edmonton, he was thrown into a city fighting a war, with hordes of military and civilian personnel going off in all directions. Not only was the city the headquarters for Alaska Highway construction but all the men and material bound for the east end of the Canol Project to Norman Wells were being funnelled through it. New buildings were being thrown up by anyone who could wield a hammer and every empty building in town was a warehouse.

He decided to blockbust his way into the hotel restaurant which was operating 24 hours a day. He was rushed to the only empty chair by a burned-out waitress who advised him to take the "special" or nothing. Sitting beside him was an army brasshat.

"I'm Oscar Grove. Welcome to Canada."

"Mike Parrot. I'm in the office of Colonel Theodore Wyman, Jr. Had to get out of that madhouse for half an hour."

"Who's Wyman?"

"He's contracting officer for the Canol Project. Moved in here two weeks ago and I'm staggered at what he has to accomplish. He thought he was going to have a cinch moving this Canol freight north until he found he had to start a navy out of a little burg named Waterways, Alberta, 300 miles from here."

Oscar burst into gales of laughter: "The U.S. Navy on the Great Slave Lake and Mackenzie River System? Ho. ho. ho. You must be kidding me." This x-rated response nettled Mike considerably but, impatient to be on his way, he said, "All right, Mr. Wise-Guy Canuck, here's my card. You show up with it tomorrow at my office and I'll show you why we need a navy in the Northwest Territories."

Oscar shrugged his shoulders. "How's he to know I'm not Hitler's cousin?" But anyway he showed up bright and early next day at the Wyman bunker. Mike pulled out a big map. "See, Canadian National Railways is the busiest place in Edmonton. It has an interchange yard with the Dunvegan yard of the Northern Alberta Railways where hundreds of cars of Canol freight are being transferred to the 300-mile branch line bound to the Waterways terminus.

"Wyman has hired a big contractor, Bechtel Price and Callaghan, to build the pipeline under supervision of the U.S. military. After the freight is dumped off at Waterways, he discovered there weren't enough Canadian boats to move it by water to Norman Wells. So he had to organize an instant navy, ship boats in and then bring in army Task Force 2600 to expedite the freight."

"Well, I'll be damned. I'd like to see your general and congratulate him."

"You can't. There are dozens of military and civilian personnel fighting to get into Wyman's office and he's in there barking out a new order every five minutes. See you later."

Oscar wondered if this genius had enough brains to make 12 decisions an hour seven days a week. He was soon to find out when he boarded a NAR passenger train to Waterways. From that small community at the confluence of the Athabasca and Clearwater Rivers, he had booked a reservation to catch the Hudson's Bay sternwheeler, the Distributor, down to Norman Wells. When he arrived June 1 he found the Distributor would arrive two days late. To kill time he hung around the office of Bert Viney, the station agent, local institution and authority on everything. This was because the NAR had despatched him to the Waterways station in 1925 when the rails finally reached town after the 12 years it took to build the branchline.

Before the war, NAR service had been light and limited to a weakly weekly mixed train. The train arrived Wednesday and laid over until Friday. This may have been slow but travel prior to that had been much slower. Bert's favorite story was about Fred Martin, a conductor who took 30 days to bring a train over the road.

"He encountered one derailment after another. That made service very informal. Another time the long-suffering Martin pulled in here September 28 and was ready to pull out September 30. But the captain of the Distributor sent word up the river by Indian runner he would arrive a day late."

"Bert, you must be ribbing me," Oscar interjected. "I thought Indian runners went out with the buffalo."

"You guessed wrong, young fellow. Indian runners were used around here into the 1930s until short-wave radio came in. But back to my story about old Fred, the conductor who sat here fuming and fidgeting until after midnight because there was an overload of freight to transfer from the boat to the train. It was 3 a.m. October 1 when he pulled out. He was standing on the caboose shaking his fist at me and cussing: 'Dammit, Bert, we come up to this country one month and don't get out of here until the next month!'"

Oscar spent the next day "casing" the town. He was jolted into cultural reality when he saw several hundred black troops who had arrived during the night bivouaced between the rail terminal and the river. He ran over to the station.

"OK, Bert, you surprised me with your Indian runner story. Are these the first Negroes who have ever visited you?"

"Yep, and you see the dining car on that 13-car passenger train? It's the first dining car I've seen in this yard. And there are 10 more trains coming to bring in 2,500 more black GIs in Task Force 2600. They are here to expedite 70,000 tons of freight down the river system to Norman Wells."

With his amazement mounting at the surprise the natty, self-confident Wyman had in store for him in Waterways, Oscar left the station to acquaint himself with the first Negroes he had ever seen. He was accosted by a dozen Negroes huddled around a fire in a barrel in long coats on a June day.

"Hey, white boy, doesn't it ever get warm in this country?" asked a sergeant fresh out of Biloxi, Mississippi.

"We can't get no sleep. The sun doesn't set 'til 1 a.m.," another added.

"We hear you have high-power beer here," came in another.

"Do Eskimos run the paddlewheel riverboats?" questioned a fourth.

They began ribbing him about the rickety NAR and all the bush country.

"There's bears in the bush," Oscar said, and he saw the possibility of meeting one really scared them.

"Did you bring Joe Louis with you?" Oscar joshed.

"Nah, we left him at home to bash all those no-good white boxers," said the sergeant. "We came here to beat the Japs."

Oscar had a friend for life with his reference to Joe Louis. Before he ambled on, they had loaded him with Lucky Strike cigarettes.

When he arrived back at the station for Bert's spin on things, Bert had another big surprise for him: a telegram. Somehow Cecil (The Bull) in Washington had tracked him to Waterways. He had a cryptic order: "Get back to Whitehorse as soon as possible. Stop. There's something you must look into. Stop."

"I have to go and pack and get outta here tonight. What's so important at Whitehorse?" Oscar asked.

"Search me," said Bert, as he ticked June 5 off a calendar.

III

Oscar was able to hitch a ride back to Edmonton from Waterways on one of the NAR passenger extras which had brought in Task Force 2600. Conductor Fat Woods had a particularly grim look.

"What we feared might happen, but hoped wouldn't, has happened," he spat out. "Those Japs landed a 10,000-man expeditionary force in the Aleutian Islands at Dutch Harbor June 3 and 4. I dunno how we're going to get the bastards out. When you get to Edmonton you'll see there's a real panic on."

"Holy Moses, what goes on in Edmonton?"

"At six o'clock June 3, 11 U.S. airlines were ordered to drop their passengers at the nearest airport and despatch every available plane to Edmonton. The order was so urgent many pilots from the 46 planes which flew to Edmonton didn't have a change of clothes. Washington did this to provide back-up to the skimpy defence forces in Alaska."

Oscar wangled a seat to Whitehorse on one of those planes in a method so secret he didn't even tell his FBI boss. As he sat hunched in his seat, a dozen images stimulated his mind. "How are my friends from the 18th building the airport at Shemya in the Aleutians faring?" he mused. "They are protected by pitifully few fighters and bombers. But now they'll finally twig to the fact those mysterious pressure vessels were for the Canol refinery at Whitehorse. Will the pipeline be built in time to move oil into Whitehorse to refuel planes when the big Alaska offensive begins?" The questions he posed sent shivers up his spine.

Waiting for his luggage, Oscar spied two bosses from the J. Gordon Turnbull engineering office having a panic attack. One had picked up a rumor that "Canol No. 1 is going to be abandoned" and the other responded "now they're talking about building six pipelines. What does it all mean?" Oscar was truly alarmed and puzzled at the Americans' sense of uselessness as he rode downtown.

Arriving at the Pig's Ear Hotel, he had a panic attack of his own. He couldn't find a place to stay — not even at Tee Cee Richards' butcher shop floor. It was booked. Nobody had time to talk to him, except ... and his mind flashed back to his last trip to Whitehorse when he was taken in hand one night by a tall brunette with the longest pair of legs he had ever wished to see. She was Coleen Patterson and she worked for a "hands-off" architect at the Sverdrup and Parcel office. This unwritten "hands-off" policy meant that nobody dated any of the bosses' women.

Oscar had thought about Coleen a lot lately and fantasized about feeling those long legs around him again. And he remembered to pick up six pairs of nylons which were brand new in Edmonton at that time. He wanted to pull a pair of them over her naked legs.

His sense of survival drove all thoughts of the Yanks and their battle plans out of his mind as he devised a manoeuvre of his own for a bed and her. She had made him acutely aware of the wartime stocking crisis. Silk stockings were a casualty of war. Some women were so desperate to appear well-dressed they stained their legs brown.

Help was on the horizon when nylons came on the market in the United States. American personnel came to Canada loaded with nylons.

Oscar's battle plan was to march on the double to the Sverdrup and Parcel office and draw Coleen into an encircling manoeuvre when she came out at quitting time. But she made a counter-attack and ran to him with a big bear hug and world-class kiss that left him speechless, except for one word: "nylons."

Her answer was: "Stay with me."

Thumbing his nose at her boss, they took off and — 12 hours later — had achieved a bedroom beachhead in war-torn Whitehorse. He trembled with desire and excitement as Coleen substituted sex for supper and he found himself in the snug grip of those long legs of hers. After a cup of tea later, he told her of the rumor he had heard there had been construction interruptus in the Canol No. 1 625-mile pipeline.

She laughed at his weak attempt at humor and said, "That is true, but my boss, Del Pound, the Canol Project architect, has come up with a new plan to beat those slant-eyed Orientals."

"I'm all ears," he said.

"Mr. Pound realizes we must provide more aviation fuel for Whitehorse, Watson Lake and Fairbanks as more fighter planes are being pressed into service to oust the Japs from the Aleutians. But he also swears the Japanese Navy will never sink an American oil tanker bound for Skagway from California. He further thinks trying to pipe oil from Norman Wells to the Whitehorse refinery is a colossal blunder."

"Sounds like he is riding off in all directions," commented Oscar. "What's his plan?"

"To abandon Canol No. 1 and use some of the pipe from it to build Canol No. 2. This will be a six-inch line laid under emergency conditions alongside the White Pass and Yukon Railway track between Skagway and Whitehorse to supplement fuel delivery by tank cars to Whitehorse," explained Coleen.

"Canol No. 2 will also deliver fuel to Canol No. 3, which will branch off Canol No. 2 at Carcross and run 275 miles to Watson Lake airport. And Canol No. 4 is a three-inch line running 500 miles to the Fairbanks airport. Comprenez?"

"No, I don't. But probably your Mr. Pound doesn't either."

(Unbeknownst to Coleen and Oscar, Canol No. 6 would come into operation in the fall as a special contract by the U.S. War Department when Task Force No. 2600 was caught by an early freeze-up of the Athabasca River system with 20,000 tons of undelivered freight to Norman Wells.)

"How about Canol No. 5?" Oscar asked.

"I think this may be a strange figment of a fictitious general's mind in a land where erratic things are done. It will probably never come off the drawing board. By the way, are you going to let me try on Nylons No. 1?"

And he did. And so to bed.

Coleen went on the attack after breakfast and Oscar couldn't keep her from trying Nylons No. 2 on her expectant legs. Before she left to display her treasure to the girls at the office she said coyly: "How about Nylons No. 3 tonight?" She left quickly before he could lasso her.

Oscar left Coleen's "cellblock" and popped into the giant U.S. Army base to see what Major Eugene Kush of the public relations staff would tell him about "construction interruptus." Although he laughed at Oscar's witty hypothesis, he played hard to get.

"Listen, kid, you think you're an investigative reporter, so go figure. I didn't tell you anything about this."

"Won't or can't?" asked an irritated Oscar.

Kush took a long puff on his cigar, gave the kid a quick wink and ushered him out. This was the signal Oscar had seen 100 times. Kush let Oscar know he was onto the truth. Coleen's data was rock solid.

Trying to sort out the pandemonium caused by the Nips, Oscar dropped into his final source of scuttlebutt, the Pig's Ear Cafe. He got talking to a man wearing a security badge with the name "William Anderson," who was cursing the mosquitoes while working on the refinery as a welder. When Oscar asked him what he thought of construction interruptus, he found out the swaggering Anderson could curse about Washington, too.

"To put it in one paragraph, I have seen all hell break loose as the result of illogical directives put out by Washington. Us pipeline welders have not been slowed down by delays, alarm and confusion and changes in orders until now. BPC is happy as hell about that. Just let me give you a birdseye view of what Washington has done to us now, however."

They moved to a back table, accompanied by rums and Oscar's handy notebook. After settling in, Oscar said, "We've both had a couple of drinks. Are you sure you've got all these pipeline numbers and diameters and sudden changes of plans straight?"

Anderson answered with a bit of an edge to his voice: "You doubt I know the reason the architect-engineers specified that a four-inch pipeline would be feasible for Canol No. 1 rather than six or eight-inch? Well, I do. It is because four large steel companies had pipe of this size ready for immediate delivery. Enough pipe for the west end had come in by sea before the Japanese attack on the Aleutian Islands. Welders were at work laying pipe towards Norman Wells before detailed terrain studies had arrived from Washington. The army brass confidently believed Canol No. 1 could be laid by October."

"Coleen told me BPC was confident it would meet its September deadline. But as my Polish friends say, things went ferschitzke when the army ordered work halted and grabbed all its welders in a panic mode to lay Canol No. 2. She also believes the completion of Canol No. 2 in record time will make Canol No. 1 redundant."

"Your Coleen keeps her ear to the ground," Anderson conceded.

"She also told me BPC, the White Pass and the Canadian government were terrified when the army ordered the pipe for Canol No. 2 laid atop the ground beside the White Pass track as a wartime emergency. Falling rocks could rupture the line and escaping oil could catch fire and a derailment could be disastrous. The Canada Department of Transport is getting ready to force the U.S. Army to bury this pipeline. Considering the decisions people in Washington are making, they must all be drunk."

"It's you that's drunk," came back Anderson in a thick argumentive tone. "I don't think burying that pipeline will ever happen. I have a friend working for a narrow-gauge railway in Arizona who tells me he is going to lose all his engines because the army is going to expropriate the White Pass as a war measure and send in a railway battalion to manage it. Rolling stock is now being expropriated in the U.S."

"The Americans can't expropriate a Canadian railway," said an indignant Oscar. "I must report this."

"You can also report that the army is breaking every rule in the book and getting away with it," Anderson said. "You should have heard BPC scream when the army couldn't find any six-inch pipe to build Canol No. 2. So the sons of bitches simply sent trucks over to the BPC yard and grabbed 120 miles of six-inch BPC had stockpiled to build the last 120 miles of Canol No. 1. The army says it's going to replace this six-inch pipe later, but you know army — lie as much as you can and steal as much as you can. But despite the 'theft' I know the over-all project will soon be resumed."

"I still think you're drunk," Oscar shouted. "I don't think you're going anywhere on this project with that bunch of twits, nitwits, dimwits and halfwits you have in Washington."

The panic the Japanese created was reduced to a whimper by the end of the month. Work on Canol No. 1 was resumed when General Somervell walked into the office of Wartime Petroleum Administrator Harold Ickes, slammed the door, roared at him for 15 minutes, walked out and slammed the door again, so the rumor went. After that, Oscar noted that Washington had begun to realize the huge size and vagaries of the Yukon and its transportation difficulties and hazardous mountain terrain.

"Gross underestimates were corrected, one being that the completion time for the Canol Project was extended to December 31. The amazing discovery was made there was no soil in most of the Yukon, so how does one bury a pipeline?! BPC was given permission to do what it had been doing all along: lay the pipe atop the ground and muskeg," Oscar wrote to Cecil (The Bull) in disbelief.

Oscar didn't especially like roistering in the Pig's Ear, the dirtiest part of the pig, unless Albertans like Jack Moore of Turner Valley came barging in to show BPC how to win the war. Jack was a big, bluff brash Canadian-turned-American welder when he signed on with a crew on Canol No. 1.

"It was 45-below when I hit Whitehorse. I was up against a head count of 30,000 coming, working and leaving a dozen Canol-Alaska Highway projects all fighting for the 600 hotel rooms in town," Jack said. "Well, by God, I didn't know what to do until I remembered a Calgary connection, Tee Cee Richards, who owned the Whitehorse Inn and butcher shop next door. But that old swine didn't greet me like a long-lost brother until I produced a crock of slivovitz from Outside. Tee Cee had hundreds of 'friends' begging him for a place to flop, even on chesterfields in the hotel lobby for eight hours. But seeing I was from Alberta he said he could put me up in the Butcher Shop Suite for $2.50 a night. Where are you staying, Oscar?"

"I've got a cellblock but there wouldn't be room for three — but never mind that," smirked Oscar. "Let's get back to Tee Cee's Butcher Shop Suite. Did he leave you hanging on a meat hook?"

"Despite the beef carcasses hanging on meat hooks, I had a really good sleep in a 3x6-foot place chalked out on the floor. Check-out time was 7 a.m., when the bellhop came in and spread the sawdust back on the floor. I slept with Tee Cee's elegant quarters (of beef) for six more nights until I got a BPC certificate. That certificate testifies I can now tack up a joint (of pipe) in six minutes. I had been using an uphand method that takes 20 minutes. They turned me over to an old-time pipeline welder named Moose Johnson from Bakersfield, California."

"Oh, isn't he the big macho trophy moose hunter the RCMP charged with for illegal hunting after he had bagged 15 moose?"

"Y'er right, but the moose in the lowland marshes were almost as plentiful as cattle. He just kept on shooting, hoping each trophy head was bigger than the one before. But he wielded a mean welding torch."

With that, Jack took off into the night to a location on Canol No. 1 so secret he couldn't even tell Oscar. That's because he didn't know where it would be himself. The project was so hush-hush he had to sign an affidavit he wouldn't know where he was going until he landed in a camp in the Yukon bush.

It wasn't until next summer Oscar saw him again. He had received a cold-weather bonus from BPC to come out of the bush to a welding job on the Whitehorse refinery where construction was behind schedule.

"Are you thawed out yet?" Oscar teased. "I am fascinated by how men can work at 60-below."

"We did all right," said Jack. "We invented a way of keeping warm. The crew lived in cabooses in a self-contained mobile camp hitched to a bulldozer. We'd drag this caboose train along beside our work. This enabled us to work 20 minutes every hour and run in and get warm for 40."

Jack settled back with a double rum and gave Oscar a rundown of Yukon survival tactics:

"The Americans had never experienced relentless, prolonged cold like this. The younger fellows were most affected as most had lived in the cities and never been exposed to the hardships nature can dish out. The older welders were a bit more prepared, having endured the swamps of South America and the Arabian desert. These older guys had thus been exposed to nature's power and had developed a healthy respect for the elements. But they, too, had a hard time dealing with air so crystalline that sound waves could carry so far it was possible to hear men talking two miles away."

"I bet you learned a lot of new secrets from these conversations," offered Oscar.

"Yes, but we always awaited the coming of the supply train to bring us information and supplies. And you could hear that damn thing coming when it was a day away from our camp. On one occasion we got more information than we really needed. It was because we had no thermometers in camp and didn't know how really cold it was. But the driver came in and told us the temperature had been down to 60 and 65-below for the past week.

"Well, when they heard that, the boys quit working then and there. They stopped dead in their tracks and refused to continue. Nothing physically had changed but the psychological effect was too much for them. They had never worked in circumstances like this before and enough was enough."

"That's one for you to tell your grandchildren," said Oscar. "How the hell did you get them back to work?"

"It took a lot of cursing to get them over their trauma-shivering. Curiously, they went back with a renewed effort, proud of how tough they were and they were going to lick nature and those pipeliners working towards them from the east in equally cold weather. We wanted to be at mid-point first and we worked tenaciously. But I was never on a job before where we had to wrap asbestos pads around each weld to allow the metal to cool more slowly for fear of the steel becoming crystalline and shattering."

"How's things going on the refinery?"

"That's a yarn for another time. Let's have another drink. I'm ready to hit the sack."

"Or go looking for women?"

"No, we got that problem solved. They come looking for us now," and Jack was on his way. "See you next Tuesday."

True to his word, Jack turned up next Tuesday with a humorous glint in his eye. "Hey, let's go down to the Yukon River waterfront where those paddlewheelers dock. I'll show you a bar where drinks are only half-price."

There, lo and behold, was a sleek 45-foot steel yacht with a 16-foot beam, a bar and sleeping for six. Captain Jack piped the boarding party of one aboard, produced a bottle of rum and told a goggle-eyed, awe-struck First Mate Oscar how he and his cronies from the refinery brought it all about.

"I'm beginning to like you and your roistering Yankee friends who are fighting for their lives yet engage in hi-jinks under the noses of the brasshats," gushed Oscar after Captain Jack ended his conducted tour.

Picking up the bottle, Jack put it under Oscar's nose and roared, "You know how much we were paying for bootleg booze? Fifty bloody bucks a crock. We held an indignation meeting to figure out how to break the bootlegger monopoly. We knew there was no liquor rationing in Skagway, Alaska. But the Canada Customs whisky sneaks shook down everybody returning on the train. Somebody came up with the idea of making a deal with the crew in charge of transshipping refinery components through Skagway. They bought Alaska booze for us, cut a hole in a pressure vessel, put the cases of booze into the vessel, packed it with straw, welded the hole shut and put a secret chalk mark on the outside. The contraband sailed through Customs on freight trains and when it arrived in Whitehorse we simply cut open the vessel and were able to retail it at $26 a bottle. That's why our social functions are extraordinarily well attended."

Enthralled by the first yacht voyage of his life, Oscar finally ventured to ask Captain Jack whose idea it was.

"Modestly, I'll claim the credit. This package was put together to solve another social problem: shortage of women. Us welders lacked the gold braid and uniforms, money and good looks, so we didn't get to first base with them," Jack moaned. "We came to the conclusion we needed some other attraction. After many committee meetings, Wailin' Eugene opined we needed a yacht; one that wasn't going to cost us any money."

Oscar guffawed even louder about this coup "thought up by working stiffs long on ingenuity but short on funds. How did you steal the steel?"

"Oscar, you know welders never steal when they can spirit things away: like 10 and 12-gauge steel as it arrived into Whitehorse. We had to enlist fellows in other departments to request other materials — like two big Mercury outboard motors. Friendly draftsmen proved handy along with Tex Pace of Houston, Texas, an experienced marine design engineer. Soon we had a shipyard going. We built a ways to launch the craft. To ensure secrecy, we solicited the aid of the refinery engineer, Jim Brady, an ex-Canadian."

"They should have put you welders in charge of this project, then this refinery, which cost $1.4 million at Corpus Christi, wouldn't now be budgeted at $24 million. Then there would have been none of these delays caused by Harold Ickes, who tried to get this project stopped, too. Is he working under-cover for the Japs?" asked Oscar.

"Ickes would have been proud to see the way we worked and launched this yacht," responded Jack. "The damn thing actually floated. Just needed some sand ballast."

After several more quaffs of the economy-priced rum, the talk turned to the scarcity of women on the Whitehorse social scene.

"Coleen is the envy of all the women in town with those new-fangled nylons," Oscar grinned.

"Why don't you bring her on the next cruise down to Lake LeBarge next Sunday. It'll only cost you a pair of nylons for the captain's lady," Captain Jack joked.

A good time was had by all and things went swimmingly. But taking Coleen proved to be a social error. The following Tuesday the welders' yacht romp came to a screeching halt when the RCMP sent out a boarding party and seized the smuggled rum.

At their next meeting at the Pig's Ear, Captain Jack morosely told Oscar, "I am a captain without a ship. The RCMP is now sailing the yacht they seized to go with the rum they confiscated. We think it was Coleen's boss, Del Pound, who blew the whistle because he wasn't invited." Nobody got away with taking any of "his women" out on a boat cruise without suffering the consequences.

"What a rum way to go. That jerk ..." was all Oscar could say. And that was the last he saw Jack for a couple of months. And when he did, it was all because Jack didn't know enough to let well enough alone.

What was bugging Jack and his Canadian fellows was a 50-cent-an-hour differential in wages below those of Americans working on the refinery side-by-side on the same job. What bugged them even more was that the Canadian Wartime Prices and Wage Board acquiesced in this obnoxious inequity all over the Canol and Alaska Highway projects.

Oscar met Jack at Fort Nelson, British Columbia, where BPC had him working on the new Kehr Military Hospital.

"How the hell'd you get here. They haven't finished the refinery yet?" Oscar quizzed.

"I'm in exile. Well, it's a long story, but you know me. I tried to use my creativity to mount a one-man protest to shoot down the Canadian-American wage disparity," he said striding up and down in a pseudo-heroic pose with his thumbs in his suspenders. "But a cop whom I met socially in Banff and whom I trusted as a friend turned me in, the prick, and BPC gave me the bum's rush out of Whitehorse to save my skin."

"I heard American welders are getting $1.75 an hour while Canadians are getting only $1.25; so what'd you do?"

"A Yank working beside me decided to book off and return Stateside. Name of William Anderson."

"William Anderson!" shouted Oscar. "Hell, I know him; ran into him in the Pig's Ear Cafe. He's a good type. What happened?"

"It turned out he was too good to me. Before he left he sold me his identity papers. So I took them over to my friend, Jim Brady, the refinery boss, and told him to put me on the payroll under my new name, William Anderson, and pay me $1.75 an hour. Brady was sympathetic and he put me on the payroll under my alias, but he told me that if I ever got caught for this shenanigan he's never heard of me before."

"What tripped you up?"

"A trip to the Whitehorse Inn to celebrate my newly gotten gains. This cop from the RCMP, Buffalo Bill Robson, came over to say hello to me and talk about Banff. Immediately his eyes focussed on this I.D. badge we were all required to wear. I saw his eyebrows shoot up. He asked me if I'd changed my name. I told him I had borrowed Anderson's jacket. He left without another word, but there was no mistaking the quizzical look he gave me."

Jack was more agitated as he continued: "A few days later I sensed someone approaching. I felt the hand of a stranger on my shoulder and a voice telling me I was under arrest for impersonating an American and dodging the Canadian draft. It was a RCMP constable in street clothes and he hauled me off to the local hoosegow. Things got pretty interesting the next day when they dragged me before the local magistrate, who just happened to be old George Black, member of Parliament for the Yukon, and a Yukon legend. He made short work of throwing out the draft-dodging charge when I showed him my exemption papers. I pleaded guilty to buying William Anderson's papers as I felt the wage disparity business warranted my own form of protest and I figured he should throw out that charge, too."

"Didn't Black find himself in a tight corner, given that he was one of the MPs who enacted this unfair law and thought you should pay a fine for breaking it?" asked Oscar.

"He took the weasel way of all politicians. He said he didn't like the law himself but, yeah, yeah, yeah, it was the law of the land and I broke it. He and the cops said I should pay $175 fine. I held my peace and didn't tell him what I thought of him and hoped I could be there to vote him out of office in the next election. But I did tell him I didn't have enough money on me as I had sent it all home a few days before. So Black asked me if I had a friend who would lend me some money. The wheels of justice turned very fast in the case so I told him yes, I had a very good friend in this court. His name was Constable Buffalo Bill Robson of the RCMP, the chief witness against me. There was an embarrassing silence. Buffalo Bill began to fidget. I had him on the spot. He paid the money."

"So does Buffalo Bill know where BPC sent you so you can pay him back?"

"No and I ain't going to tell him. Case closed."

Jack's recital of his adventures with the cops tickled him. He was the kind of character Oscar liked to cultivate as Jack never suffered fools kindly. He took pride in his work and his other accomplishments. He was good enough that BPC made him an inspector on a special crew on Canol No. 1 to ensure nothing would impede the flow of oil under 1,200 pounds per square inch into the Whitehorse refinery by April 30, 1944, the day of the official opening. He was hard at work when Oscar ran into him again, checking for breaks in welds, line blow-outs and obstructions, one of which was a very dead rabbit.

Oscar had finally wangled a trip along the new Canol road directly from Whitehorse to Norman Wells in a command car. The FBI was highly indignant at the wastage Jack pointed out to Oscar — and Oscar reported Jack's words verbatim to Washington.

"BPC sent a real dodo from Texas in here to run this crew — a tall ex-football player. He was responsible for me nearly getting burned alive in a crude oil fire near the pumping station at Mile 221 West. We came across a break which had spilled about 1,000 barrels of 41-gravity crude into a coulee. Tex told me to cut out the broken section with a torch and install a pup joint, which is a kind of eight-foot-long sleeve. I suggested a better way as I knew if I went out there and struck an arc with a torch there'd be a helluva an explosion, one cooked welder and a forest fire.

"My way wasn't the way they did it in Texas and Tex got on the new telephone line and called Press Nibley, the superintendent, and squealed on me. While Press was sympathetic to my complaint, Tex came off the phone and told me to get my helper to help me put on a set of leathers, a large sheet of canvas and a tank of carbon dioxide to spray on me if I caught fire. Well, whatta you know? That goddam oil exploded and slammed me into the oil covered ground. I screamed and scrambled out and ran to the truck, grabbed a jacket to put over my head while my partner wrapped me in the tarp and turned on the carbon dioxide. The fire didn't get me but it was a close one. It did burn up three trucks and millions of acres of bush for a couple of weeks. I found all six-foot-four of Tex down on his knees pounding the ground with his fists in frustration.

"This was not his only bad decision. In a previous incident, his bad judgment resulted in three new bulldozers being lost in a muskeg two miles wide and seven miles long. A catskinner was nearly drowned. Tex found it easier to order bulldozers into, rather than to go round, the muskeg. That was too much wanton waste for even the Americans, so they shipped him back to Texas."

After that "indignation meeting," Jack gave Oscar an admiring look. "You're going to be one of the few Canadians to travel the entire road. It's a spectacular route across the Richardson Mountains, but it's not a well-built road. It will fall to pieces pretty quickly after the war — starting with mud slides and floods washing out bridges."

"Well, I hope this doesn't happen. This is a great trip for me as, two years ago, there was no road and I had to fly around by Edmonton," said Oscar with some awe.

Oscar's return trip over the road left him in a bit of a state. He had picked up a rumor that oil was not going to reach the refinery by April 30. And he wondered if that could be a nail in the refinery's coffin. He picked up another bit of gossip that after the oil started running, Sverdrup and Parcel would pick up stakes and return to St. Louis, Missouri, likely taking Coleen with them.

He was even more dismayed that she didn't give him the usual bear hug when he showed up at the cellblock. Instead, she was in a great state of excitement and shoved a book of lottery tickets under his nose. She held in her hand the strangest lottery ever held in Canada. The grand prize would go to the person whose guess was nearest to the time the first barrel of oil reached the refinery through the pipeline Jack and his buddies had tacked together.

"Oscar, write down April 17 on that ticket," she commanded. It was only after Oscar had plunked down $1 for a ticket that Coleen grabbed him and began whispering secrets.

"Oscar, Oscar, I've missed you so much. And, Oscar, I've another secret: about Major Parson's big goof. Major Parsons, the area engineer, turned up at our office in an agitated state mumbling about the oil coming to a stop 150 miles east of Whitehorse. A field report had come in that oil had been slowed to a mile an hour as the pumps couldn't force it over Horsedung Mountain any faster. He was moaning to the boys that the calculations on his slipstick showed that oil would never reach the refinery by April 30. He was in a helluva state until Del Pound came wandering in with his sly grin and said: 'Major, your slipstick has forgotten to tell you the last 120 miles has been laid with six-inch pipe.'"

As Coleen further recalled it, "Parsons let out a University of Waterloo engineers' cheer, 'Yes, and this will allow the oil to flow faster as there is less friction in the six-inch. Yahoo! Everything is going to be hunky-dory.'"

When Coleen was finished describing Parsons' epiphany, Oscar asked, "So you think the first barrel will come sooner than the ticket-holders assume?"

"Yes," Coleen answered simply. "Now it's time for us to have that big Easter ham Tee Cee Richards brought in especially for me."

Three nights later on April 16 at 8:15 a big brouhaha broke out. The first oil had arrived. Bells, sirens and shouts were heard all over town. Parsons bought a round for everyone at the Pig's Ear. Two girls came running to Coleen and told her another girl from the office won the $2,500. Tickets had been sold as far away as the Pentagon in Washington.

Back at the cellblock Coleen said, "Sit down, Oscar, you've also won a jackpot. I've been hired for a job at the Public Roads Administration. I will be here for another two years."

Now it was Oscar's turn to trap her in another bear hug. Later as they relaxed, Coleen was curious about the large number of notebooks he had filled at Norman Wells. "What is going on there? How could a small trading post on the Mackenzie remain anything but that?"

"That's a good subject for a seminar tomorrow. I'm tired out with all that excitement going on here," he replied sleepily.

IV

On his first trip to Norman Wells, Oscar's notebook showed that bungling on Canol No. 1 was four times worse than anything he had seen in Whitehorse. He noted down hesitancy, dithering, secrecy, wrangling between the U.S. military and civilians and justification for continuation of the project. He found it disheartening.

The location was so far inland from the fighting in the Alaskan Archipelago that the American forces found it hard to realize they were fighting anything but black flies.

"I heard them constantly cursing a pipeline which was supposedly a subordinate subsidiary of the Alaska Highway Project, but seemed so remote from it as to be useless," he wrote. Later, when he returned and was reading these notes to Coleen, he stammered over his scribbling so much that she took the book from his hands and said fondly, "You're like all reporters. You can't read your own writing and don't know how to spell. You'd better let me type up these notes or your biographer will make you look like a dummy. Remember, you've likely got one of the biggest events in the history of the Northwest Territories in here."

She took the notebooks to the office and typed them out one by one and brought them back to the cellblock at night for a review of accuracy.

"You say you had a streak of luck when you walked into Ted Link's office at the Imperial Oil refinery there?" Coleen queried when she brought the first notebook back to the house. "By the way, who is Ted?"

"Sorry I forgot to tell you. Dr. Ted Link, an old Northern hand, was despatched from Toronto by Imperial to take charge when the U.S. Army decided to build the Canol pipeline. In fact, I give him credit for getting the project off the ground. Twenty-five years previously he was sent in there to set up the refinery. He assured the Americans he could supply them with enough oil from the wells to supply the Whitehorse refinery."

"So he is the Canadian kingpin at Norman Wells? And he was glad to see you?" pursued Coleen.

"You bet. He grabbed me by the hand and pumped it and told me how glad he was to see a Canadian come into his dingy digs. He kept looking over his shoulder as if a blustering U.S. Army engineer was about to burst in and retail him another tale about the escalating civilian-military power struggle. Poor old Ted seemed to think the Yanks were running around like chickens with their heads cut off and were driving him nuts."

"Wasn't he a bit hard on us Yanks?" countered Coleen archly. "Didn't Link realize the capture of Dutch Harbor in the Aleutians by the Japanese scared the pants off the Americans in this battle zone?"

"I think he did," mused Oscar. "But he had been trying to tell the American 'idiots' from Day One that Imperial Oil could supply the Canol refinery with 3,000 barrels of crude per day if they would give him 10 geological survey parties to locate further supplies. At first, they listened to him, then they started listening to their number crunchers telling them the Japs could be licked without spending money to locate new supplies of oil."

"I see in your notes where you asked Link why they didn't enlarge the Norman Wells refinery and pump aviation gas to Whitehorse rather than moving crude oil through Canol No. 1."

"Yes, I did. And he had no simple answer. He then handed me a historical outline of the Norman Wells refinery and told me to take it away and study it and come back. You know, he is the Yanks' key man there. General Somervell gave him credit for being the first Canadian to show him that Imperial Oil could supply petroleum either way."

Coleen's eyes widened at these revelations. "The Yanks must have driven him nuts. Only a fool would hand you these classified wartime papers and allow you to take off with them."

Oscar responded with a self-satisfied grin. "You can find papers in the briefcase also indicating Norman Wells is in the big league as Imperial Oil is a subsidiary of the giant Standard Oil of New Jersey. I'd like to have seen the faces of those slave-driving hot-shots from Standard Oil if they ever found out I was walking around with a top-secret copy of their Norman Wells battle plans. Cecil (The Bull) tells me he is going to give me a raise for this coup."

"Think of the irony of this little girl from Elgin, Texas, kissing the first spy to operate in the Northwest Territories 1,300 miles from nowhere." She laughed and laughed as Oscar practised walking tip-toe spy-style. "Let's review these plans and put our stamp of approval on them."

She began pulling papers out of his briefcase and reading aloud: *"Imperial Oil built this small refinery in 1925. By 1940 the refinery had been expanded to 800 barrels a day to supply gasoline for the Eldorado radium mine at Port Radium on Great Bear Lake and the gold mines in Yellowknife. Later, to accommodate another increase in demand that was developing with the opening of the Fort Nelson airport, more wells were brought in and that included six more this year."*

"Here's another exposé about your friend, Link, and Fred Bimel, an executive of Standard of New Jersey, opening secret negotiations with the U.S. military for all the oil Imperial Oil can supply. Link was so confident he can supply 3,000 barrels a day he told the military to get out its moneybags and make a deal. Oscar, do you really think Link's positive posture has been the deciding factor for giving the green light for the Canol Project?"

"Well, all I can say is what he told me when he came bursting into my hotel room that night with the rest of that story. He somehow found out that Somervell's boys looked over eight locations in Alaska and Canada and all of them were useless. Then Somervell pulled a slick number by asking Link for a written report on Norman Wells. This report went straight to President Roosevelt. Somervell knew precious little about our location; indeed, some of the mountainous terrain had never been traversed by white men. But Link assured him he could put together a wildcatting program for more oil and that seemed to be all the assurances Somervell needed to pass on to Roosevelt."

"And you think Roosevelt rubber-stamped Link's report?"

"Oh, Christ, yes. Roosevelt not only did that but he gave Somervell a top-secret classification for Canol without asking Somervell for a master plan. That classification meant nobody, not even the FBI or the opposition senators, could pry into his expenditures." Came a titter from Coleen: "And the FBI decided to try to trap Somervell by sending you here to do it?"

"If you say so. But Somervell had enough smarts to write in a cancellation clause if the wildcatting crews found no more oil. Another piece of fancy footwork was that the American military put out its contracts to civilians on a cost-plus-a-fixed-fee basis. This meant that Imperial Oil would have all the wildcatting information in its geological reconnaissance records for free."

"Why is my Uncle Sam handing out all these sweetheart deals to you Canucks? You are in this war, too!"

"I realize that, but if you will remain quiet for the next two hours I'll give you my speech from Link's point of view. Harrumph. Tsk, tsk. Link believes he is dealing with a foreign nation whose national policy seems to be to spend its way into winning a war of retribution that hit at its own shores. The Americans have reached the point where they are now schizophrenic and paranoid. He doesn't know where he stands with them. For example, the secrecy they put on the project was so tight none of the Canadians knew that Norman Wells had been designated as the eastern jump-off point for the Canol pipeline and the accompanying service road. Although this is one of the top landmark construction projects in engineering history, Link is completely flabbergasted at the number of changes in direction. He had sent his plan to Roosevelt for wildcatting approved one day then seen it postponed the next day."

"I can't understand why Link couldn't fathom the logic of us fast-moving and quixotic Americans," Coleen said softly.

"Wait until I tell you about this guy, Glen Ruby, he has to put up with. Ruby works for Harold Ickes, the U.S. Petroleum Administrator for War. Ruby got on his case when Link had gone back to Toronto after the project was postponed. Ruby somehow figured that, despite the postponement, the wildcatting program should go on. He therefore called Link and asked him to fly to Whitehorse to contact (or con) General Patsy O'Connor to OK the wildcatting program right away. Link demurred that he couldn't get an airline priority to fly into the war zone. But Ruby used his guile to get him there by buying a ticket in the name of 'Brigadier-General T.A. Link'." Which brought a delighted squeal from Coleen: "Oscar, what outrageous fable are you going to tell me next? Making your friend an instant general. Isn't that fantastic?"

"It gets better," Oscar continued. "Link's mission to O'Connor was successful, but it was a pyrrhic victory of sorts because soon after Link started putting together a bunch of geological survey parties, he found himself in the middle of a power struggle between Harold Ickes and War Minister Henry Stimson of the U.S. Ickes sent Ruby to Norman Wells to spy on the military as he alleged the army insulted him as if he were an outcast. The general refused to make him privy to their secret oil and gas contracts. Everyone laughed like hell when Ickes got off a one-liner, "Just because I don't wear a uniform the Stimson crowd thinks I might be spilling my guts to Mr. Hitler."

"This is about as bizarre as things can get," sighed Coleen. "This sniping and viciousness and warfare is going on despite the fact we are in a shooting war with Japan. How in the hell can we win a war under these conditions?"

"Curiously, Link felt the same way as you until a couple of shrewd Canadians arrived in camp engaged in the preliminary work necessary to opening a new oilfield. Fred McKinnon came in from Calgary to lead one of the 13 geological exploration crews Link said he needed to work out of Norman Wells. The other was Anton K. Money, a surveyor who had made a living as a trapper at Ross River, Yukon, for 20 years. One night I ran into him in the bar where he was engaged in drinking Outside greenhorns under the table and boasting that none of the geologists was going to traverse a mile of territory until he had finished his work. A large hoot of laughter and razzing broke out at this chirpy little bastard with the funny name and I couldn't hear all that he said. I grabbed him on the way out to his room. He told me if I could find him a bottle of bourbon to bring it along the next night and he'd explain what running a baseline was all about," said Oscar.

"You could only pick up that putrid stuff from an American," Coleen sniffed.

V

Coleen was up at six demanding Oscar drink his coffee and give her the notes he had made on Anton K. Money.

"I'm glad Anton liked that bourbon you gave him. I didn't think any low-life American would bring that rotgut to Norman Wells when over-proof rum is available."

"Yeh," Oscar answered sleepily. "He had his hotel room temperature at 90 and he was bundled up in his parka. He froze his tailbone every day in January leading that baseline survey along the Mackenzie River. That is one mean river. The survey is required by the geologists before they can start their work. The heat in his room was the first time he had been thawed out. He claims to know why that old bozo, Dangerous Dan McGrew, whom Robert Service wrote about, flung himself into the fire-box of a river steamer to get warm. After a final shiver, Anton looked searchingly at me and asked if I could keep a secret. Then he opened a big folio of maps. Good God, he was showing me top-secret maps for oil exploration for the whole Canol Project. We could have been court-mar-tialed by Colonel R.W. Lockeridge of the Northwest Service Command. But fortunately Lockeridge was in Edmonton, we hoped."

"The irony of you being a spy makes me shudder," said Coleen.

"I was keeping my eyes averted so I wouldn't let off a big guffaw," responded Oscar. "He was showing me a map covering an area in which the Canadian government gave the U.S. War Department the rights to search for oil under special permits. Incidentally, those maps the war department obtained from Ottawa were inaccurate and useless and had lit-tle resemblance to the areas they were supposed to represent. That's why the survey was necessary. The designated area is bounded by the Arctic Ocean on the north; a line 75 miles east of the Mackenzie River on the east; the 60th Parallel on the south; and the Alaska-Canada border on the west: a tremendous piece of real estate, don't you agree? This piece of

Canadian land area was handed to the U.S. for an oil exploration as long as the war lasts. Nobody else is now allowed in it."

"How did Anton fit into this picture?"

"As I understand it, his job was to 'run' this 400-mile baseline from Fort Wrigley to Fort Good Hope. Then aerial maps are made from the baseline he ran. These maps were handed out to the geologists to take their surveys off."

"I know something about such things, working in an architect's office. Why did we need such a long baseline?"

"As I said before, you Americans didn't know where you were going and it was your style to map terrain thoroughly. I nearly jumped out of my skin when Anton told me that Sverdrup and Parcel and J. Gordon Turnbull were the ones hiring the 11 teams to do the work under his direction. I couldn't help telling Anton that's where you worked and you knew most of the Canol secrets. No doubt you wrote all the letters to all the surveyors you hired in California. Guess what he said about you? He told me I am the luckiest bastard in the North. You are the kind of woman every man on the Canol Project would die for."

"You guys; can't keep your mind off women — even when you're supposed to be licking the Japs," snapped Coleen. "I saw these young surveyors come in from California and I groaned. None of them had ever seen the cold and snow they were expected to work in. Most had never seen a dog team nor been on snowshoes. But I have a sharp eye for men. Not one of those I hired ever got hurt and not one of them quit. I guess a few froze their fingers."

Oscar smiled. "That's something to write home about. Let me tell you what your men were up against. The first thing they discovered was an unusual winter phenomenon on the Mackenzie. The river valley was filled with finely powdered snow blown by a 30-mile wind straight from the Arctic Ocean. They were thus working in a perpetual snow storm. Up on the bank, 200 feet above the river, it could be 40-below but there's no blowing snow blasting your face. It makes quite a sight to be standing on a lovely clear day to look down into a whirling white mass that completely covers the river.

"As hard as the blowing snow was on the men, it was even harder on the sled dogs pulling their gear. The men could pull their wolverine-trimmed parkas across their faces and peer through the long guard hairs, similar to looking through a mosquito net. But the dogs didn't have this kind of protection. The snow blew into their eyes and coated them with ice. The mushers had to stop periodically to allow the dogs to get their backs to the wind and claw the ice from their eyes; also chew the ice out of their toes.

"What if they had to stay out overnight?" queried Coleen.

Oscar got that wry look in his eye: "If you'd like a clinical demonstration about that I'll show you. They carried small silk tents big enough for two or three men. They also carried little stoves which were rarely used in the tents because they made sweat. They snuggled into eiderdown sleeping bags whose insulation prevents cold from penetrating. Want to give it a test, Coleen? The human body is the world's best heat generator. Put two or three together in an eiderdown, that doesn't let the heat escape and you've got a fire going, even at 60-below."

"I didn't know you were a dirty old man. Now get your mind back on this story about how U.S. taxpayers' money was used by Anton Money to complete this gigantic project he undertook," commanded Coleen in mock-seriousness.

"Anton's real trick for keeping warm is never to allow a sleeping bag to rest on snow. Use an air mattress or spruce boughs between the bag and the snow. The bag won't be lumpy if the spruce limbs are arranged with the points up — a good spring mattress."

"His notes also showed each crew consisted of an instrument man, two helpers, an Indian guide and a dog musher. It was the job of each party to place markers on strategic mountains for their own triangulation from the river to make them visible for airplane pilots during aerial surveys. The markers also had to be placed to be seen by the surveyors from at least two points up and down the river. The markers were flags set up on permanent standards. Beside each flag was a colored board, the lumber for which had to be carried up the mountains on the backs of the surveyors."

"Evidently Anton was out there freezing his butt off. What was the occasion for that? I thought all the work was being done by my men from California," said Coleen.

"It was Anton's job to find the camps each of the survey crews had set up for taking astral observations, pinpointing from regular star-survey procedures. He visited each party once a week bringing supplies and receiving the information they had accumulated and saw that it was projected onto a plane table survey. More interesting and exciting to me was the next step, although I didn't understand most of it: how experts from the University of Kansas, the U.S. Air Force and Canadian Pacific Airlines worked together. They used the information Anton brought in to produce aerial maps of the gigantic area. The aerial maps were developed into trimetrogon maps of the main rivers running into the Mackenzie. Placing the trimetrogon maps under a stereoscope, it was possible to learn a great deal about the geology of the river basins before the ground crews went in to make further examination. Isn't this wonderful?" Oscar said in awe.

"Oh, but we have some smart Yankees on this job. We are on the cutting edge of this new science to make it possible to find oil in a godforsaken area of Canada," Coleen gushed. "I remember my grandfather used a stereoscope to produce three-dimension photos to amaze us kids. I bet those geologists were happy to have the two sets of maps they were issued."

"I know Fred McKinnon was. He was newly graduated as a field geologist from the University of Gumbo at Chancellor, Alberta. He wanted desperately to go into the mountains to try out this new high technology. He had been in the Royal Canadian Navy waiting to sink German submarines, but Link used his influence to get him seconded to stay in Canada to fight Japanese. That's where I ran into him during a familiarization course in Norman Wells. It was in May and the snow was still on the ground and his crew was working with something I never expected to see."

"And what was that? An early hatch of black flies?"

"No, it was black soldiers who were impressed by the top American engineer into sweeping snow off the rocks. The snow was driving the geologists crazy and that's the only way they could figure to get on with their work. Sweeping didn't work. So they just had to wait a month for the sun to get rid of the snow. Your Yanks didn't know a damn thing about this northern climate."

"I'll concede that grown men sweeping snow was pretty stupid," said Coleen.

"I'll say it was, but it didn't equal the stupidity of keeping those black soldiers there all winter. I found out they were a company from Task Force 2600 which I had seen arriving at Waterways a year previous. It made my heart bleed to see they were billeted in windowless stinking shacks huddled around stoves, terrified by the cold, all along the Mackenzie River system. Fred and Link were as outraged as I was, keeping those GIs from the Southern States doing nothing all winter. I sent a signal to Cecil (The Bull) in Washington about this outrageous waste of human resources. He blew a gasket about this fiscal atrocity, the old curmudgeon.

"I guess Link tried to atone for the mistake by suggesting some of those black GIs might be used as cooks for the 13 geological survey parties during the summer. A meeting was called but when they learned they'd have to go out in the bush and sleep in eiderdowns, one of them stood up and said: 'Dr. Link, I'd like to know if there is any danger connected with this mission?' There was a dead silence. They were never used in the bush they feared."

This drew a compassionate reply from Coleen. "They probably thought it was beyond their competence since the woods were full of bears and I heard bears frightened them to death. And I would think some of them must have been talking to Anton telling some of his stories about freezing his butt on the baseline survey."

"I think the Negroes would have done all right in the field. The 65 men in the field parties were a mixed bag of Canadians, civilian geologists and American oil company geologists who came in from all parts of the world. Most are sub-surface geologists completely clueless about roughing it. The helpers are summer students, few of whom have had experience in field geology, and had to learn how to cook for themselves or starve. You know, root, hog, or die.

"A couple of days before Fred was airlifted to his first assignment to the headwaters of the Engineer River in a bush plane, I tried to con him into taking me along to do a feature story on this historic oil search. Well, you know what happened. He told me he was sorry he just wasn't equipped for carting greenhorns on 30-day tours along the whitewater rivers he expected to encounter. Secrecy wasn't a concern; surviving was. So I was grounded, dammit. But he wished me better luck in the next war. He tried to mollify me by sending me a copy of his daily logbook at the end of his tour. Of course, I've never received it," he said with some annoyance. "So what is new!?"

"Oh, poor Oscar," said Coleen, ruffling his hair. "You know very well this lip service happens to every reporter. But you're a spy. Fred likes you and he'll catch up with you yet as he and you have a bond; a great sense of history in this virgin territory of the Northwest Territories. Now what else can you tell me?"

"The drill devised by Link for despatching crews from Norman Wells was to equip each with a tent, grub, canoes and those ultra-confidential maps, plus a special northern survival pamphlet which all were required to read. Caches of supplies were left at strategic points along the river beforehand. The main gospel for survival was canoes should never be left on a riverbank without being weighted down or tied down as sudden gusts of wind can blow them away. Also, the rivers in this area are unstable and rise more quickly than those in Wisconsin. As Link predicted, a crew from Wisconsin ignored him the first trip out and arrived back exhausted from a long walk after they watched the canoes float away. Each crew floated down the assigned river and was picked up on the Mackenzie and flown to another assignment."

Two nights later, Oscar came bounding into Coleen's cellblock with a big brown envelope.

"Coleen, Coleen, where are you? It's here. It's here."

"What's here? The latest copy of Esquire?"

"No. No. Fred's logbook. What adventures he's had on the three rivers which he toured. His adventures are as well-written as those by Gordon Sinclair in the Toronto Star. I can hardly wait to tell you about his tour of the Arctic Red River. His party was in there 42 days and in all that time never saw another white, brown, yellow or black man or even a Martian. They were completely isolated with no radio to hear if the Northwest Territories had been attacked by Japanese commandos. He prayed every night nobody would break a leg. A plane was supposed to check each party once a tour, but the check was the exception rather than the rule.

"It was screamingly funny to Fred that the top American army engineer got the idea the mountains were full of spies. A bear had visited camp one night and broken into a wooden box of those trimetrogon maps. Water had gotten into the obliques and ruined them. He was disgusted and threw the useless maps away to lighten the load. When he returned to base, this engineer was furious at the loss of the photos. He figured they'd fall into enemy hands. He accused the startled Fred of feeding the precious maps to the bears and, until more sensible heads prevailed, was going to send him back and recover the remains from the bear droppings; then bring the pieces back to Norman Wells and paste them together. What do you think of that?"

"I'm quite positive Fred had to write up a report which will end up in the U.S. Army Archives," Coleen joked. "And I've just picked out another funny story about Fred and the naked geese. Around the end of July, his crew paddled around a bend in the river and found themselves in the middle of the biggest flock of Canada geese they ever saw. They were all naked, just like a nudist colony."

"Pray tell. How come?"

"This time of the year adult geese go into a moult and the young ones haven't developed feathers — and neither can fly. The geese began to swim to the river banks and scramble into the trees — but not before they caught a few. Greaseless goose was a welcome change from the horsecock they had been eating."

"Now, look who's talking dirty!"

"I thought you knew, Oscar. That's what all the Americans call that endless supply of Spam in their C rations. What a dummy you are at times. Fred was so happy with roast goose he threw away some of the horsecock for the bears. He had roasted the geese with dried carrots and potatoes from the C rations. As he and the boys sat around the campfire after the meal, they began recalling other wild birds they had chased around college dorms and other unusual meals. He had managed to wangle a meal at a Buck Valli Drilling Company grub shack on the Engineer River. They had all kinds of steaks and chicken and green veggies he hadn't eaten in months down south due to rationing. The cook also boiled up some vegetable called broccoli which he had never tasted before. He also heard some of the drillers bitching because no grapefruit or peanut butter had come in. But when the tea came in for these Americans, the cook threw it away — and that's what Fred's crew was drinking that night as he saved it from the garbage. Americans can't operate without peanut butter, and no God-fearing American will drink tea. What other eccentric events has Fred written down in his logbook, Oscar?"

"He claims their hours were about the same as a piano player in a whorehouse because of the midnight sun. It only set for about two hours a day in July. Listen to his story about what happened to the crew July 6 when the second plane set down on a lake a mile from the river with 750 pounds of provisions and the canoes at 10.30 p.m.; it was still daylight:

"We worked on cutting trail and moving our stuff on our backs to the river. By 8 a.m. July 7 we had half of it there, so we set up camp, had breakfast and went to bed at noon. Nobody stirred until 11 o'clock that night, then woke up and had another breakfast. From 1 a.m. to 10.30 a.m. July 8 we had moved all our stuff. At noon we started getting things organized. At 8 p.m. we had a fish supper and hit the sack at 11 p.m. bone-weary. On July 9 it was raining so we didn't get up until 11 a.m. We left camp to traverse a 2,200-foot mountain at 1 p.m. We reached the top at 2 a.m. July 10. We hiked back to camp by 5 a.m. It was to bed at 7 a.m. and were up for breakfast at 1 p.m."

"What other sections of Fred's log amuse you?" Oscar demanded.

"I like the fact Fred is a good housekeeper in the bush; that as a party leader he insisted that the boys take a day or two off once in a while to clean up and not become slobs. He worked them pretty hard and they were entitled to take time to rest up. It is his experience that those who stay dirty in the bush usually brought back poor reports. He felt that just because they were away from the bright lights of civilization there's no reason to live like animals — so they always shaved, kept clean, washed their clothes and kept the gear in good shape. The cleanliness habit helped them overcome the drudgery of being wet so often. When working along a river they couldn't stay dry; they were wet most of the time. They got to the point they'd walk out into the water first thing in the morning because sooner or later they'd be lining a canoe or making a portage. All socks were washed with a washboard. The guy who had washboard duty once decided to shorten the drudge by putting them in a river with a rock in the toe and floating them all day. That didn't work as they were so full of silt nobody could walk in them. Goodness, Oscar, there's enough good material in here to write a book."

"I suppose so. And then there are many entries in Fred's log about the dangers of canoe upsets that scared even experienced outdoorsmen on these unstable mountainous rivers. I'll read you one scary incident in which Keith Huff and Ian Crawford were getting out of their canoe and it got away on them. Fred found it half a mile downriver full of water. They managed to recover everything, but all their clothes and bedding were soaked. Wet clothes were bad enough, but wet bedding was even worse. Life jackets were useless and were never used on this project. In the cold northern waters they were redundant as it takes more than a good swimmer with a life jacket to survive. Wetting the food was even worse. In another upset a 20-pound bag of sugar turned into a 30-pound liquid mess. Another upset revealed Ian couldn't swim. He was fortunate. Keith dragged him ashore after he was dumped from a canoe by tree branches. Fred found others couldn't swim. But all 65 returned safely."

Oscar and Coleen spent six days reading log books on the geologist's harrowing experiences and close calls. But the greatest denouement was the oilfield proved to be a gigantic dry hole!

Afraid Cecil (The Bull) wouldn't believe him, Oscar sent Fred's logbooks about the wastage of all that money to Washington. But not a peep was heard from him. Oscar was astonished.

"Why didn't that dummkopf, Cecil (The Bull), pan the army for this huge wildcatting failure?" he asked with a furrowed brow.

"It's just that you tight-fisted Canucks can't understand the equinamity for the possibility of losses on huge gambles, even in wartime," Coleen explained. Cecil (The Bull) became a fair-haired boy in Washington as he saw to it that Fred's logbooks made the rounds as "history in the making by us Americans."

"Somehow I feel depressed after going through the excitement of Fred's wildcat program that its failure could result in closing down the Canol Project," Oscar said after six beers. But she was optimistic:

"You can console yourself this isn't the first or only loss on the Canol Project. Just cast your mind over the big trouble Colonel Wyman ran into in that small village of Waterways."

"Yes, I'll have to go and check that fiasco very soon," he said before dropping off to sleep.

VI

"How long are you going to be away?" Coleen whispered when Oscar woke up next morning and started packing.

"As long as it takes me to find out what has gone haywire around Waterways this fall," said Oscar, loosening a pair of arms that could easily keep him in bed until 11 a.m.

"Like your city editor used to tell you, 'keep it short' then." From under the mattress she pulled a report "which I copied at the office for you. It says plans called for the delivery of 70,000 tons of freight to Norman Wells before freeze-up. However, 20,000 tons got frozen in on the Mackenzie River system as early as mid-September. This has put schedules at Waterways behind those of Whitehorse and Skagway. That is, when those beastly civilian bosses in Washington aren't putting roadblocks in the way."

"Hey, you're beginning to sound like a politician," Oscar said appreciatively. "But the real trouble was God. He froze up the northern waterways a month early this year and threw schedules out of whack. This early freeze-up caught everybody by surprise. Once the deep-freeze sets in there is no way of moving anything except by air or tractor-trains. Those forces who came in from navigating on the Mississippi River (which seldom freezes) were completely in shock."

"I wish I was going with you, Oscar, to see this phenomenon. You'll write me about it, won't you?" she said anxiously.

When Oscar's first letter came, she found him dumbstruck not only by the heavenly phenomenon of ice but by a sociological phenomenon. "The sociological phenomenon is that this project is in the hands of two groups of men who are at war with each other: blacks and whites. I've never seen anything like the microcosm of life in the southern United States that is being replayed in this remote Alberta village of Waterways. Now I have an idea what racial segregation is all about. The friction imported to

Waterways became so troublesome that Wyman had to put a river between the black and white camps by moving the white forces across the Clearwater River to Fort McMurray. Even after that, there was more friction than freedom when the whites and blacks hit the beer parlor at the Franklin Hotel. To keep peace, the army had to declare alternate 'black' and 'white' weeks. The saw-off was backed up by military police.

"One day Wyman came into the hotel dining room with arms akimbo, a familiar stance, and barged into a black MP in the doorway with a rifle and an order to keep out all white military personnel. I heard him say, 'Black boy, get out of my way.' But the MP was having none of that. He told Wyman this hotel was 'off limits to the Yew Ess Army — and you are sure Yew Ess Army.' Wyman beat a hasty retreat before this military logic, remembering to his chagrin he had himself cut the order banning army personnel. He had shown up a week previous with his wife and found the dining room crowded with black GIs as it was 'black week.' He had been unaware of the saw-off and thought it was 'black week' all the time and he had to get rid of the blacks."

Oscar added a postscript to his letter: "The handful of residents of Waterways were fully cognizant with Canada's participation in the horrors of war on the European front. However, in their wildest dreams there never had been an expectation their hamlet would metamorphose into a giant 24-hour-a-day U.S. military post with the arrival of Task Force 2600. What I have said above in this letter will demonstrate the fact the little community has been momentarily paralyzed, dumbfounded and outnumbered in a sea of uniforms. A logistician and stranger by the name of Lieutenant-Colonel Wyman has become a czar. He is masterminding the huge flow of freight to Norman Wells with what appears to be no-nonsense certainty. It is interesting to see how quickly things settled down, with the villagers taking things in stride."

Just when things began to settle down, the villagers found themselves thrust into a maelstrom of frenzied top-secret activity that few could make head or tail of. A disquieted Oscar sent a signal to Cecil (The Bull): "We are now inundated by waves of rumors and speculation. It's an entirely different ball game than when I left here last spring in a hurry to go back to Whitehorse."

Cecil (The Bull) got back to Oscar: "What's with this Wyman? Is he turning out to be a jerk who can't inspire his troops to get things done on time? What's he going to do about all that undelivered freight?" Oscar shot back: "The easy-going people here don't know what to make of

Wyman. He's a short, self-important type who's inclined to strut around with a chestful of medals." To which Cecil (The Bull) chuckled, "That's a start to being a bit of an ass."

"All I can say," was Oscar's weary reply, "is that he's an engineering genius who doesn't suffer fools, varmints nor the weather, but ignoring the weather might be a bad mistake. I have his aide, Mike Parrott, on my list to pump for information. He's turning out to be as good a source of secret information as my friend, Coleen, so I'll get the dope you need as I know Parrott is fond of Hudson's Bay Jamaica rum."

Oscar first decided to quiz the friendly station agent, Bert Viney, who worked 20 hours a day at top speed as he had two jobs: one, doing the paperwork at which he wore a pair of specs at the end of his nose, and the other, wearing a black conductor's cap which had "NAR" embossed on it, chasing around the yard keeping track of train arrivals. He was proud of his work and excited about his achievements on the war's front line. Pulling Oscar aside he said, "Let me show you how these combative Yanks do things instantly that take us weeks to do. See this new siding? Because there was no help around here, as most of the men were called up by the army, I hired old Bill McRuer and his horses to lay the siding to cope with the extra freight trains. He was on the job a week and was getting nowhere until one day, without a goddam word being said, the U.S. Army unloaded a big bulldozer off a flatcar and the job was finished before nightfall."

"This is real fast-tracking, eh, Bert?" Oscar chuckled.

A bit crestfallen, Bert expostulated, "Was that bridge across the Clearwater River there when you were here last summer; the one which the NAR has been talking about building for 10 years? No? Well, those omnipresent Yanks showed up on each side of the river and, as us locals gazed open-mouthed, they completed that bridge in 10 days."

And Bert wasn't too "goddam busy" to tell Oscar with delight how "my American friends are causing gridlock by putting 35 to 70 cars of freight into this goddam yard and I'm working overtime sorting out this gridlock. There are no warehouses either here or in Fort McMurray and we are seeing GIs working overtime piling goods onto rude platforms and 'pinching' tarps to cover the clothing and food supplies."

"I hear you are even stopping trainloads of pipe on the main line outside of the terminal and unloading them there?"

This sent Bert into a paroxysm of cussing some more: "You're bloody right we are. We have to, for instance, because idiots at Central Supply in Columbus, Georgia, rushed 500 Fresno road building machines up here three months ago. They're neatly lined up in a five-acre lot beside the main staging area. They were never used."

"Bert, I hear an order has come along to ship them back next week."

Bert was building up a head of steam. "Hell, yes, even that pair of hotshot assistants Wyman got me from the New York Central Railroad were buffaloed when they saw a two-acre lot filled with half-tracks which have never turned a wheel." He spat the tobacco he was chewing to the ground. "I never fathomed why other idiots sent an express car full of specially trained dogs here to run messages along the Mackenzie River in winter. They were sent home, too. There are enough sled dogs howling around here without them."

Spending some time one afternoon with a Big Rock Warthog Ale in the bar, Oscar mused about Bert being so much dismayed about the Yanks' careless spending in time of war. He came to the conclusion that it was practically useless for the FBI and the opposition politicians to try to ride herd on the outrageous bill the taxpayers faced for the obscene cost of arms, ammunition and frivolities. He left the bar at 7 p.m. and saw a long line-up of men with thirsty looks on their faces at the freight shed at the NAR station.

"Jeez, is the war over and everybody is buying tickets to go home?" he wondered aloud and decided to join the line. Arriving there, he found Bert wrestling with a roughhouse crowd picking up their monthly ration of a crock of liquor which had come in on the afternoon train from the Alberta government liquor store in Edmonton.

"These liquor shipments are my biggest bugaboo. The Alberta government doesn't want to see anybody going to war drunk so it makes liquor hard to get and I have to get a signature for each of the 624 crocks that arrived here today. And that wears me out."

Bert wasn't the only person in Waterways working 140 hours a week. After the last bottle was signed out, Bill Bednar burst through the door to hassle Bert about a late train. Bert introduced Oscar to Bednar, a hard-nosed young petroleum engineer from the University of Oklahoma who had been sent in to expedite freight for Wyman.

"Old Bert here has been telling me you have been causing traffic jams on the senile NAR," Oscar twitted him.

"What a miracle this beat-up railway has been. Bert and his master maniacs have dumped so much freight in here on me it looks like I have created the biggest bottleneck on the whole Canol Project," responded Bill heatedly. "Well, it isn't my fault, because the planning done in

Washington required Wyman and me to have all this freight delivered to Norman Wells by September 1. It just isn't going to happen."

"That mighty industrial machine in the United States is pointing the finger at this little hamlet of Waterways for holding up the whole war effort," Oscar pointed out.

Bill answered him in scientific thoroughness: "The industrial complex in the U.S. had no trouble filling the needs for the Canol contractors. U.S. railroads were able to deliver thousands of cars to the Canadian National and Canada Pacific yards in Edmonton. But nobody told me there were no Canadian barge fleets on the Mackenzie River system and when I got to Waterways I run into this roadblock. Loaded cars of freight have been backed up all the way to Winnipeg. What a let-down," he roared. "None of these Canadian river transporters, whose boats were built in Noah's day, wanted to increase their bottoms for fear they'd be stuck with them after the war."

"What was the matter with those pontoon rafts the army tried to use to move freight?" Oscar put in.

"None of you Canucks thought of telling us about the ferocious storms which lashed Great Slave Lake with 20-foot waves. Neither did you tell us about the treacherous, shifting sandbars and low water in rivers waiting for the deep-draft barges and tugs Wyman brought in from the Mississippi. So what I am really doing here is building a navy yard. Some jerk from here evidently accused a couple of senators of financing a second U.S. Navy in outer Canada," Bill rumbled, and stopped to light a stogie.

"Cripes. Neither did you-all tell us about this freeze-up coming in the middle of September. I don't see how we can deliver all this freight before next June. We had to let out a special contract to build 74 steel barges in Waterways in our navy yard and bring in some tunnel-shaft tugs with shallower draft."

"Oh, oh, I wonder who gave that information to the senators?"said Oscar, nursing a quiet grin.

That off-hand remark really got Bill pacing up and down the floor lighting into Oscar about the U.S. war effort "using prison labor, nominally chain gangs, working in boat yards in Kansas City creating the 'Canuck Navy' by building barges and river freighters then knocking them down and shipping them to the little-known port of Waterways. We now have a fleet of 175 barges, 14 utility boats and 34 river freighters and tugboats sailing the Mackenzie 1,300 miles to Norman Wells!"

"Welcome to the Port of Waterways, Admiral Bednar," Oscar said giving him a salute.

Bill pulled out his engineer's slipstick and made a few calculations: "I would estimate that 26 million good American dollars are being spent on this American fleet sailing wholly in Canadian waters. I further estimate it is costing $1,000 a ton to transport the freight to the east end of the project."

Oscar was speechless. Here were some figures that could blow Cecil (The Bull)'s suspicious mind. He lost no time in forwarding them to Washington.

The kid from Picture Butte was also speechless when he learned of the existence of a 15-plane air force set up with landing strips along the Mackenzie and the new Canol road. Head office is in Fort McMurray. It is a bush plane outfit pressed into service by the Canol management contractor, Bechtel Price and Callaghan. As he related his discovery to Cecil (The Bull), he pointed out "it was developed out of necessity by imagination. There are no roads, no radios, no phones father north — just a few Indian runners and bush pilots flying by the seat of their pants. And they are helping to defeat Japanese kamikaze pilots in their Zeros. You should see some of these old wrecks in the Canol Air Force. They are flying junkpiles," he said with awe.

This brought a wry comment from the scabrous Cecil (The Bull) that "we have been assessing some of these off-beat reports from you and we may have to cut your ration of Canadian Club rye."

"Cut the crap, Cecil. You know I don't drink rye. My drink is overproof rum and I am always right. All the looney-tune projects on this project will go down in history." Nursing his imagined hurt feelings, Oscar wrote to Coleen "some facts about the Canol Air Force which you will some day be able to tell our grandchildren. Bob Randall, a legendary northern bush pilot came aboard and was upgraded to chief pilot in charge of assembling a marvellous fleet of 15 antiques to establish Canada's most gung-ho airline. He had the geriatrics flown to Edmonton to a repair hangar shipped in from Los Angeles by BPC. One real prize was a plane said to be flown by Jacqueline Cochran in the London to Johannesburg air race in 1933. Another was used by Howard Hughes to film 'Hell's Angels.' One was a Ford Trimotor in good shape which piled up at Billings, Montana, and killed the crew. From the Sperry Rand Corporation he picked up a little Bellanca Airbus which had seen a lot of sky and, on a flight for the Canol Air Force in July, saw 55 miles of the Slave River.

"Joe Irwin, another of the bush pilot fraternity, was at the controls with 15 passengers aboard to Fort Smith. At 8 p.m. it accidentally dumped all its oil and, with what appeared to be rakish aplomb, he made an emergency landing on pontoons on the river without scaring his fares to death. A pontoon barge from the Canuck Navy hove into sight and Randall arranged a tow at three knots an hour through the land of the midnight sun to Fort Smith. Arrival time was 6 p.m. next day. That was a white-knuckle part of the trip for Irwin as he was fearful he would be seen by his flying buddies and razzed about the ignominious situation for the rest of his life. He turned steward and served passengers Slave beef stew (purloined from survival rations) in gallon tins."

Some time later Oscar received a letter from Coleen: "Your humor is priceless. But you must be thunderstruck by the imagination and wild and woolly mayhem my people used in their frantic push to move freight through the Waterways bottleneck. And about your remark about 'our grandchildren,' you must have a real crush on me."

Oscar noticed the bottleneck attracted frequent visits from Wyman. He heard the boys in the bar bitching about the colonel being a martinet and driving his people relentlessly, although admittedly he got things done. Wyman's biggest defender once was one of his own men, the bespectacled studious Mike Parrott, his aide. He was so upset by all Wyman's bloopers, he wanted a transfer. "I can't stand that bastard always getting into trouble by bawling hell out of his subordinates in public, making arbitrary decisions and putting on temper tantrums, then expecting me to come along later to smooth things over. The guys hate his guts for his kind of military arrogance that resulted in the Pearl Harbor debacle."

"But from a professional point of view he is an engineering genius," Oscar again pointed out.

"That's the bad part of it. Left to his own devices, he can get things done. But the politicians and military brass in Washington drive him crazy. And he, in turn, drives me crazy. You know, I would like to send you to Fort Smith so you can see a piece of engineering Wyman did that eliminated a bottleneck that has existed ever since the white man began navigating the Mackenzie River system as the chief trade route to the Northwest Territories," Mike offered.

It was not until after the freeze-up Oscar made it to Fort Smith, Northwest Territories, population 260, which had been swallowed by 1,200 black soldiers from Task Force 2600. Oscar was able to make the trip because he discovered the president of the Canol Air Force was Matt Berry, an old bush pilot and friend of his family. Matt had been hired by

Wyman for his knowledge of the North and had been put to work locating new landing strips along the Mackenzie River system and the Canol road. Oscar was delighted to find Mike on the flight, too, and Mike was able to show him the Fort Smith bottleneck from the plane.

"You see that 18-mile granite bar in the middle of the Slave River, making it unnavigable. All the cussing about that nuisance stopped one day when Wyman stopped in. He ordered some gigantic cranes be placed at each end of the granite bar. The barges of freight are now lifted out of the water, loaded onto rubber-tired floats which are pulled across the portage then slung back into the Slave at the other end of the bar. Their cargoes are not unloaded."

"Well, I'll be damned," exalted Oscar. "Up 'til now the Canadian river transportation companies had to have two sets of boats, one at each end of the rock, unload the freight, then have it portaged across the rock and reloaded. Wyman forever!"

"Unfortunately," said Mike, "despite all his genius and the use of advanced technology, Wyman is on the point of being defeated in his quest to deliver all the freight through these roadblocks. Ice has been forming on the river system and I think he knows he's about to be defeated by the cold of a Canadian winter. He's facing demotion if he doesn't make good."

Oscar's attention was diverted away from Wyman's jackpot by what he considered a more serious one of his own. The hotel was double-booked.

"I'm sorry, we have 50 carpenters in here sleeping two or three to a room," manager Paul Kaeser said, but when he saw how distressed Oscar was he managed to bunk him in with a sergeant, one of 35 army personnel in there, too. He also told Oscar why those carpenters were as distressed at being here "as you are trying to get a bed. They were being moved to Norman Wells by boat, but when the freeze-up came they were stuck here. They can't get a priority on the Canol Air Force to fly them out yet."

"A helluva way to run a war," Oscar offered.

"When the army started receiving bills for their lodging after seven weeks, they sent an officer in to investigate, but he came out shrugging his shoulders."

Oscar took great delight in sending a report to Cecil (The Bull) on this snafu and Cecil's sentiment about running the war was the same as his only he called them "goldbrickers sitting around for months doing nothing. That's preposterous."

On the return flight Oscar was delighted to see Matt Berry at the controls. After some bantering, Oscar told Matt, "I feel a bit sorry for Wyman. He must be in a black mood these days."

Matt didn't say anything for a few minutes, then he pulled Oscar by the coatsleeve and said, "I know a few things about this country and I have suggested one which may save Wyman's skin. It's going to cost him a bundle, but I think he can get most of that 20,000 tons of freight to Norman Wells six weeks before the ice goes out in the spring."

At that point the plane ran into turbulence and everyone hushed up "and so," Oscar reported to Cecil (The Bull), "I haven't found out yet what Wyman is going to do. But I will — if I don't freeze to death in the attempt."

VII

"You'll never believe the change in my boss, Colonel Wyman, since your family friend, Matt Berry, president of the Canol Air Force, paid him a visit a few days ago," Mike Parrott told Oscar, as he knocked back a double Hudson's Bay Jamaica rum in the officers' mess in Edmington one blustery day in October. Then he knocked back another. Oscar had never seen a prolix Mike look so effulgent.

"Did my friend, Matt Barry, bring Wyman an epiphany?"

"He sure as hell did," exclaimed Mike as he ordered another. "The harried colonel was sitting looking out the window watching lusty Edmington with a jaundiced eye day after day with his hands in his vest pockets repeating over and over again, 'This gigantic mess I have on my hands could only have happened in the Northwest Territories,' wondering how he could appease his superiors in the U.S. War Department in Washington. Washington was down his neck harder than Tokyo.

"In his despairing black mood, he had convinced himself Canada's unforgiving cold weather had broken his spirit. He cursed his luck, the Japs, the natives and God in heaven for allowing the natives to thrive in this misbegotten weather while it was defeating the giant American mechanized army with which we expect to win this war. But, glory be, that all ended the day Matt came in to see him."

"Yeh, Matt told me he had a suggestion to lay on him," Oscar murmured.

"As Matt left, Wyman let down his stiff military bearing. He literally hugged Matt and I thought he was actually going to kiss him. He came bellowing down the hall roaring like a drunken sailor from the U.S. Canuck Navy in Waterways.

" 'Why didn't you bastards tell me about this?' Wyman hollered at me and anyone else in earshot. 'What's wrong with you sons of bitches?' He was beside himself with delight. He was now going to deliver that 20,000 tons of freight frozen in on the east side of Great Slave Lake."

"All right, out with it. What did Matt tell Wyman that made him jump?" Oscar asked.

"Simple. Matt told him the ice on the Mackenzie River system on the west side of Great Slave Lake goes out six weeks before the ice on the lake and the rivers east of it where all that freight is frozen in," explained Mike.

Oscar looked puzzled. "What's that got to do with anything?"

"Wyman says it has everything to do with moving all the freight from the east side of the lake this winter to the west side of the lake to a staging area which he will build at Axe Lake, which is on Mills Lake near the confluence of Great Slave Lake and the Mackenzie River. The key thing to remember is that in 24 hours Wyman had been transported out of his dismal stupor and he has put in motion what he calls Canol No. 6. Matt played a part in the new plan by advising Wyman to place the staging area at Axe Lake. He had observed from years of flying over it that this location was perfect as the water current along the south shore of Mills Lake would keep a deep harbor scoured out. Isn't that neat?" beamed Mike.

"It looks like Wyman realized the answer to his own question: the natives regard snow as a friend, not an enemy. He could use tractor trains and trucks to get the jump on the 1943 navigation season to move freight on the frozen ground or across the ice of Great Slave Lake just like the Germans went around the French Maginot Line with their tanks," said Oscar. Later that day with a full head of steam, he wrote Coleen:

"I foresee the day when Canol No. 6 will be known in engineering circles as one of the most fascinating stories of courage and ingenuity in the transportation history of Canada. Wyman's ingenious scheme involves substituting tractor trains for railway trains, moving freight over existing Canadian winter roads and building hundreds of miles of new winter roads. In addition to the tractor trains he will throw into service every kind of truck he can muster: from four-wheel drives to grain trucks driven by Alberta farmers. Trust you Yankees to put your engineering genius to work on such a problem."

Mike was so proud of the gigantic chess board reaching 1,300 miles from Edmonton to Norman Wells that he sneaked Oscar in to view it. "You can see it's extremely complicated. The plan today — or segments of it — may be abandoned, modified according to weather conditions or treated as a Canadian myth. The need is real, albeit costly," said Mike.

A billet-doux from Coleen indicated she was puzzled about tractor trains. "What in heaven's name are they? We never saw them around Kansas City."

Oscar enlightened her. "They are made up of cabooses thrown together on an assembly line basis. They are really small boxcars which can also be insulated and equipped with stoves and sinks to carry a crew. When mounted on heavy-duty sleighs they can be used for transporting all kinds of freight, including perishables. Any number of sleighs can be chained together and pulled by a bulldozer. Cabooses also solved a big problem when hundreds of civilian personnel flocked into the new Peace River railhead. Even though the army built mess halls to accommodate hundreds, took over an office downtown, built a 1,000-foot loading dock and dozens of bunk shacks, there never was enough sleeping accommodation until Wyman purloined some cabooses from somewhere and set them up at the railhead. They could sleep eight nicely in double bunks — if there was plenty of ventilation. Soon I may be riding a tractor train from Peace River to Axe Lake, where some of the cabooses are being used for temporary housing at the staging area there. I'll send you a report on the stink quotient.

"I am quite intrigued," Oscar continued on page two of the letter, "that the chess board schematic of Canol No. 6 has taken on the appearance of a color-coded spider web. Wyman has drawn in lines from the location of frozen-in freight that must be moved to Axe Lake. Web No. 1 begins at Waterways, follows the NAR branch line back to Edmonton and continues along the main line from Edmonton to the pertinently named little town of Peace River. Here the freight is transferred to the new staging area and reloaded onto tractor trains for the 450-mile trip to Axe Point. Toodle-oo."

Oscar was off on the Edmonton-Peace River passenger train the next day. Alighting from the train, he heard someone call his name and there was his friend, Herb Viney, from Waterways.

"Herb," Oscar cried, pumping his hand, "how the hell did you get here?"

"Well, Oscar, after months of 20-hour days at Waterways, I collapsed from exhaustion one day. The NAR finally decided I was overworked and kicked me upstairs. I was transferred here to help out. And for the life of me I find it incomprehensible why my friend, Wyman, put this new railhead here."

"I was wondering that myself as we came down that steep winding grade into town. Why didn't he put the railhead 12 miles farther west at Grimshaw rather than this dangerous place for locomotive engineers to move trains in and out of?" wondered Oscar.

"Locomotive engineers have always cursed Peace River. Coming in from the east, there's that steep grade you found: the tracks drop into a cut

500 feet deep. One hundred yards west of the NAR station there's a bridge over the Peace River which does double duty as a highway bridge, then there's a westbound hill seven miles long to go up. It takes hours to get a train in and out of here with these small steam engines," Herb explained, and he continued to nag. "Once the freight is unloaded at Peace River it has to be loaded on tractor trains which haul it to Grimshaw. Once there, sledding is easy for 100 miles over an all-weather road, known as the Mackenzie Highway by the locals, then it is necessary to continue along a winter road another 350 miles north to Axe Point."

"Where are all those bulldozers coming from?" asked Oscar. "Cecil (The Bull) would like to know why nobody in Canada can buy 'dozers for love nor money yet Americans can order them in by the gross."

"They are the result of Wyman magic. He managed to get top-priority requisitions through Washington and, as you can see, hundreds are being unloaded at Peace River. They are also needed for building all the winter roads, too.

"Here's something else you may not know about winter roads. The less-critical supplies will be stockpiled at Axe Point and barged to Norman Wells in the spring. Some of the perishables needed at Norman Wells will be sent right through in trucks or tractor trains over a winter road now being finished. Isn't that remarkable?" exclaimed Herb. "These winter roads are very rough and they are the width of two bulldozer blades wide knocking down the trees."

"I was talking to some people on the train up here and they told me with typical Northern pride they've been able to teach the Yanks a few tricks about building winter roads," Oscar said. "I guess they've supplied Yellowknife for years over the Mackenzie Highway which is a winter road."

"You must have been talking to Buck Shaw about how he and his winter road crews learned to use bush pilots to ferry mechanics and parts to them as well as keeping the crews happy by taking in mail, grub, tobacco and some fresh fruit to keep them from getting scurvy," explained Herb.

"I really liked Buck's story about how to keep anti-freeze from freezing," returned Oscar. "He was working under a straw boss from the Northwest Territories Road Department by the name of Judd Brehaut. Judd was a control freak who gave the boys a pain in the ass. One day at 65-below a bulldozer stopped dead. They found the radiator plugged with frozen anti-freeze. Buck got into a big row with Judd as Judd ordered the relief driver to take the dog team back to Indian Cabins to buy some better-quality anti-freeze. Buck just melted the frozen anti-freeze, added 40% water and the mixture never froze. Old Judd was flabbergasted to learn lesson No. 1 about northern driving."

As much as Herb griped about the pushy brash Americans he had come up against, he always handed out praise where praise was warranted: "I am going to say right now that nobody but a bunch of damfool Yanks — pushed by a vicious enemy or not — would have the bravado to tackle something most of the native northerners tried to tell them couldn't be done. This has happened time after time. Look at those people downtown. I bet only a handful know what's going on outside the town limits or what it's like to face this fiercely cold weather on a road dubbed by one of those bulldozer drivers as 'a road never built for travel of any kind: tractor trains, trucks or any other vehicle made by mankind.' That driver headed a tractor train that took a month to reach Norman Wells after leaving Peace River, one break-down after another."

Being a product of the 1930s depression years, the only thing Herb could not countenance was the way Wyman did everything "at any cost."

"He won't get the results he expects," Herb warned. "By the time he gets through moving all this freight, the equipment and supplies needed will cost more than the value of the freight. I estimate it will require 23,000 barrels of fuel on this project alone. There are also three or four other projects on Wyman's chess board which, as you tell me, are denoted as the arms of a spider web. The supplies he needs will also include hospital facilities, lumber for camp construction, warehousing, floodlights, laundry equipment, food and emergency supplies."

It took Oscar over a day to find enough warm clothes and winter boots to enable him to sign on as honorary bull cook with Tractor Train No. 42 out of Peace River March 15 bound for Norman Wells. He reported to George Midgeley, the day foreman. George had been helping to train tractor-train drivers, but had been told to drop everything and head out that night. He could see Oscar was a greenhorn, but he wanted to make him welcome. "Just to make you useful as well as ornamental, I'll give you a job nominally assigned to me — writing up the train's daily log book. You can write, can't you?" he grinned.

The thought that ran through Oscar's head at this "fortunate" development was "Oh, for the joys of a snooper." He opened the log book and found the crew consisted of 16 catskinners, two truck drivers, two Imperial Oil employees in charge of perishables, a bull cook and Angelos

Milanos, the Canadian cook, who turned out to be the hero who often put in 24-hour days. He also noted a remark by George that "every crew working in such close contact develops natural inspirational leaders." In this case it was "The Three Musketeers": C.L. Allison, who is Aramis; F. Shandel, who is Parthos; and W.W. Davidson, the thoughtful Athos. "I expect whatever job they do they will be resourceful and ambitious in their leadership," George wrote in a footnote.

Oscar liked George's philosophy about the job and wrote about it in a letter to Coleen: "As we stood watching a group of black GIs throwing perishables on the last of seven cabooses, George told me these guys have no idea where Norman Wells is, nor do they care. Their biggest worry is in keeping warm in this bloody awful cold. Half an hour at it and they are ready to drop everything and hurry back indoors. They've thrown on our load in six hours. Since they don't know where it is going to end up, why bother with the details of whether it is ammunition or eggs? They have their orders and the best way to carry out orders is to get these huge stockpiles out of sight. Like the sins of man, the departure of each train to them is absolution into the limbo of forgotten things."

The other cabooses of the train were two of building materials, two of prefab bunkhouses, a supply sleigh, a kitchen and one loaded with spare tractor parts. Motive power was two bulldozers and a snatcher to pull the others out of the ditch if need be.

Tractor Train No. 42 developed a personnel problem which plagued it from the second day out until it reached Axe Point March 27. The big boss brought in a weasel named S.F. Fox, who announced he was there to take charge of the train, with no other explanation. His first action was to demote George to night foreman. He also announced he intended to run the train 24 hours a day with an objective of 55 miles daily.

"I'm glad Fox didn't take my job of keeping the log book away from me," Oscar told George. His main entries were that they never made more than 15 miles daily and cooks kept quitting after tiffs with Fox. George described him as a "prick of misery." Also in the "prick" class were BPC construction crews which achieved the superlative stupidity of creating a lack of snow for the tractor trains to run on. They built miles of winter road, then forgot to push the snow back onto the roads. The frozen gravel on the roads burned the steel runners off the sleighs.

After the first two nights of gut-wrenching interminable miles in a caboose with the hard-working crew of Train No. 42, Oscar was ready to bail out. Then he began to think of the alternatives, such as retreating back to the Picture Butte Bugle writing obits. No, he wanted none of that. If the rest of that gung ho crew could suffer stiffness and sore spots, so could he. If they could ward off the rigors of the hostile bush in front and the Japanese military from behind, so could he. He decided to wait two more days; then two more days came after that. But then a wonderful thing happened and he decided to continue to Axe Point. The sous-chef made a huge pecan pie, something he had never eaten before — but he ate two pieces with gusto. From then on pecan pie made him forget frigid, long-drawn-out days, shortages as a way of life and the rock-hard assaults of S.F. Fox.

Oscar quit cussing his frozen feet when one bright day Axe Point showed up. He saw the wharf 210 feet long which could handle two barges at once when the navigation season opened on Mills Lake. The barges would haul stockpiled pipe and other freight out of a vast clearing stretching a mile back from the lakeshore.

In another letter to Coleen, he wrote there were two things he'd never expected to see there. One was that amid the barrels of gasoline, trailers, machinery, knocked-down Nissen huts and vehicles, there were two cabooses full of barrel stoves which had never been forwarded to Norman Wells — stoves that were badly needed by the Negro troops stationed there. The other was finding a hot shower, laundry and washroom with hot and cold running water, modern plumbing, three electric washing machines and tubs. This was the lap of luxury and lush accommodations the rough-and-tumble crew never expected to find nearer than 2,000 miles. They were sorry to leave this remote battlefield stop-over at Axe Point with its radio station, hospital, mess hall and workshop after three days. The camp workers lived in bunk shacks and Nissen huts. It was the rule of the camp the tractor train crews could sack out in the workers' beds in the daytime. The main form of recreation, after eating food that was rationed in the rest of Canada, was a winter road put in shape so they could bundle into a station wagon and travel 10 miles out and back again; reminiscent of driving down Leahy Road in Portland, Oregon, or Sylvia Starzyk Strasse in Chancellor, Alberta.

The road to Axe Point was good in comparison to the road the rest of the way. A sign on the bulletin board revealed the 115 miles to Camp 18 were "fair," 278 miles to Blackwater Lake were "bad" and 250 miles to Norman Wells were "horrible."

"This letter is being posted in Peace River. I decided to hitch a ride back with two Alberta truckers, Earl Hacking and Lowell Caldwell of

Cardston. Their two beaten-up trucks gave me a rockier ride than the tractor train. Hugs and kisses."

Coleen wrote back to tell Oscar she had read his letter three or four times and he was heartened when she told him, "I showed your letter to some of the fellows in the office. They termed this a long historical ride over the budding Mackenzie Highway. I also liked your idea of asking George Midgeley, the night foreman, to send us a copy of his log book on the rest of the trip."

With the prospect of returning home, Oscar and the two Alberta truckers were in good humor for the 24-hour non-stop trip to Peace River.

"So you're making some hard, cold cash?" quipped Oscar.

"We had to do something after closing up our General Motors agency. The company quit sending us new trucks," said Hacking. "We didn't make much money the first trip as we ran the engines 24 hours a day to keep the radiator from freezing up. Then a GI arranged to get us some anti-freeze from company stores for $10."

"You appear to be operating short of anti-freeze and short of sleep?" Oscar speculated.

Caldwell spoke up, "One of the guys was telling me he never went to bed two nights in a row on a job like this. I used to wonder what in hell we were doing out in the middle of nowhere driving a jalopy like this. I think it was the element of danger that kept us awake, even though we drove in convoys of five or six."

"We don't think those damn Japs work as hard as we do!" cut in Hacking.

Oscar was about to reply when his head hit the roof of Hacking's 1938 Dodge truck for the 500th time before arrival in Peace River.

The first person Oscar met on his arrival was Mike Parrott. "You'll be glad to know I heard by the latrine-o-gram that your boss, Fox, on Train No. 42 was given the bum's rush off that train at Blackwater Lake. He and a truck driver were given 40 minutes to evacuate the train."

"I'd like to have seen that," grinned Oscar. "When I was at Axe Point I saw freight arriving over the ice from Fort Fitzgerald and Fort Smith. Is this another spider web on Wyman's Canol No. 6 contract?"

"Yes. Briefly, this is a gigantic contract which calls for a 290-mile winter road along the south shore of Great Slave Lake. It will make history in the Northwest Territories if Wyman does what Matt Berry wants him to do," replied Mike.

"And that is ..." queried Oscar.

"Upgrade this spider web of Canol No. 6 into an all-winter road. This road would enable the water transportation companies to bypass the Fort Smith portage and the trip across treacherous Great Slave Lake," Mike explained.

"That would really change the face of northern transportation," Oscar said matter of factly.

"Except, I don't think it will happen," winked Mike. "Wyman has a deal with Mickey and Pete Ryan, the Fort Smith portage operators, and he doesn't want to upset it for some strange reason."

Navigating over the ice of the huge lake in winter was almost as wicked as the waves were in summer. "I have seen 30-foot ice pressure ridges that required detours of 50 miles or by bashing through the ice and waiting until the water froze over again. Giant snow drifts, blizzards and white-outs also hampered progress.

"Oh, by the way, did I tell you about mustering the Canol Air Force to move two barge loads of alkylate frozen in the Mackenzie River at Camsell Bend, 250 miles south of Norman Wells? This alkylate is used by the refinery to mix with regular gasoline to make 87-octane aviation gas. Lack of the alkylate threatened to ground the Canol Air Force which was being used to fly in perishables and other supplies to Norman Wells."

"Where did they get the regular gas for the planes?" questioned Oscar.

"Oh, that came from the Imperial Oil refinery at Norman Wells. There was no use trying to move in the delayed shipment of alkylate by dog team; it was too far. Wyman solved the problem by throwing himself at the feet of Phil Lucas, the farmer, who learned to get himself out of jams on the farm by doing the obvious everyone else had overlooked. That system worked well when he and his pal, Harry Marsh, a locomotive engineer, joined the Canol Air Force and were assigned Norseman aircraft. The military flyers from the U.S. had often chuckled at the rural rubes from Alberta. They figured Norseman aircraft were only useful as passenger planes to fly three or four visiting generals around. They couldn't see them as planes which would move much freight," said Mike.

"The wiseacres watched slack-jawed as Phil and Harry took off at 8 a.m. when it was still dark in the northern winter and headed for the barges which they reached at 10 a.m. daybreak. They landed on the lee side of an island where there was some snow for their ski-equipped planes about a mile from the barges. Indians were hired to haul the 45-gallon drums by dogsled. They were able to load Phil with five barrels, quite an overload. It took two weeks to do the job by making two trips a day. Both were happy it was over as it was pretty risky flying. The people at the ground stations were pretty happy during the flights, as the U.S. Transport Command had installed radios in the planes. The pilots could bring the news-starved people news from Outside."

"This is one of the most unusual stories I have run into on this trip. I think the fact Phil and Harry were the chief Outside line of communication is pretty touching," said Oscar. "How did they get left there? I presume all these Americans on the ground were GIs from Task Force 2600 who were building the airstrips Matt Berry located for them."

"Yes," said Mike. "For instance, 50 GIs from the 89th Engineering Regiment at Fort Wrigley had not been able to complete their airstrip before freeze-up. These poor guys, mostly from the Bronx, and never out of a city before, and their lieutenant (from Missouri) have been there all winter. Phil got to know them well as he flew in there all winter with fresh beef, pork and vegetables to supplement their army rations. One day on his alkylate run, the lieutenant radioed Phil he had a man with a broken leg. Could Phil stop and pick him up? This put Phil on the spot as he was overloaded and there was a big frozen bump on the runway. But he used all his bush-flying skills to land and take off and in two hours the patient was in hospital in Norman Wells.

"Phil's a great Canadian and I think those GIs are going to put him in for a Medal of Congress for coming to their aid in another crisis. They had run out of cigarettes for two weeks and the lieutenant pleaded with Phil on the radio to try to find some or he'd have some suicides on his hands. Using his farming skills, Phil forgot to unload six cases of smokes he was delivering in a shipment to Fort Smith. Then he got on the radio to tell the lieutenant help was coming. He thought the lieutenant was going to crawl up the microphone in gratitude. The 50 GIs came running out to the plane and in less than 30 seconds everyone was smoking. They had no control. They were just crazy for a smoke. In half an hour one of the cases had disappeared," Mike concluded.

As Mike prepared to take off, Oscar said, "Give my regards to Colonel Wyman."

What Mike said next shocked Oscar to his roots. "Sorry, Oscar, but Colonel Wyman is no longer in Edmonton."

In a high state of agitation, Oscar shouted, "Mike, what are you telling me? What is happening? Doesn't anyone care about winning this war any more? Wyman couldn't have been that nasty."

"The only thing I can tell you is Washington sent a rules stickler by the name of Colonel George Horowitz with a big rulebook to do an inspection of Wyman's command. He filed a terrible report which was placed on my boss's file — and he is now toast. He was transferred (or banished) to Fairbanks and has been replaced by General L.D. Worsham."

This brought forth another anguished response from Oscar. "Poor Wyman. He is another victim of the unforgiving Canadian North; worked his heart out to achieve a mission impossible."

With that he and Mike parted sadly contemplating if the failures in the field were the result of stupidity in the army high command.

Down at the mouth, Oscar went to the Peace River NAR station to buy a ticket to Edmonton and bid his friend, Herb, goodbye. Opening up to Herb, he said fiercely, "Why didn't the U.S. War Department shut down the entire Canol Project rather than just can the officer-in-charge? Don't you think he engineered a solution to his problems in an acceptable way? Why did they come down so hard on him? Why is Brigadier-General Somervell and the command keeping this project alive when it appears to be going nowhere? Did Wyman know something he shouldn't have been privy to?"

"Yes, something makes me think this whole project is developing into an enigma," sympathized Herb.

"Maybe I should be talking to Coleen again about this. She keeps track of all the inside stuff," Oscar mused.

Arriving in Edmonton on a fine spring day, he found things busier than Wyman could ever imagined they'd be. Busy as they were in Edmonton, he heard things were simply booming in Waterways with 3,000 civilians and military personnel working feverishly to untangle the blockade that had become Wyman's nemesis. Barges were being built and launched at the U.S. Canuck Navy yard to move the rest of the freight into Norman Wells.

Oscar found a situation that the Canadian government said would never happen but was in full swing. The U.S. Engineering District found itself desperately short of help in the 500-seat mess hall and appealed to Canada's National Selective Service. This federal government body made a ruling that kids 16 and over could go north to work without having to write final exams. Bob Shepp and 13 other pals from the Jack Gorman High School in Hanna persuaded their parents the wages of $150 a month plus board could make them fortunes.

Oscar found himself sitting next to Bob and his group and 300 other young bucks riding the NAR passenger train to Waterways. They all ate

Lac la Biche whitefish three times on the slow trip over the unballasted line that slowed the train to six miles an hour over track built on muskeg.

"Ever heard of the U.S. Canuck Navy of Northern Canada? That's whom we are going to be serving grub to," laughed Bob.

"That means you'll be up at 5 a.m. seven days a week slinging hash, mopping floors and carrying out garbage. Let me know how you get along washing dishes, too," commanded Oscar.

Seeing Bob on the street a week later, Oscar saluted him and told him to report.

"Them damn dishes gave us more problems than we expected, but eating is culture shock, sir. Nothing's on ration. We get to help the cooks make home brew in the back kitchen. I have a certificate saying I am 21. I had to do that in self-defence. We have a guy who is a great baker, a great cook and a great bootlegger. He said he would kill me if I didn't get a liquor permit and give it to him to buy liquor for his bootleg trade.

"My other big difficulty was short-arm inspection. After we all stripped to the wrist watches these hard-boiled army nurses came in to give us shots and they were pointing and laughing at us, the horny bitches. I wasn't one of the ones they picked for bunkhouse patrol."

"What do you do when you aren't bootlegging? Do any of the workers get anything to eat?" asked an amused Oscar.

"Oh, I'm on the hospital shift right now," Bob answered hastily. "I was chief dietician there for a while. When I found a patient who needed a steak to improve his diet, I'd requisition two 12-ounce T-bones from the cook, fry them up and we'd have one each."

"How did you make out washing dishes? Did anyone ever complain about grease on his plate?" Oscar enquired slyly.

This sent Bob into a paroxysm of cussing about the hell-hot-kitchen where he worked a few weeks and "the worst part of it was we had to work fully clothed at all times. I couldn't see how a few drops of my sweat would get washed off onto the dishes and poison anyone. And one day I was working in that steaming hot kitchen piling dishes onto the conveyor belt to the big dishwasher stripped to my undershorts. I could see somebody poking his head through the swirling steam; when it came closer I could see he had a brass hat with gold braid.

"So I hollered, 'What can I do for you, Mac?' And back came the answer: 'My name isn't Mac. I'm Colonel Foghorn Avramenko from the Medical Corps. The first thing you can do for me is go get to hell out of here and don't come back without shirt and trousers.' I put up a fuss, but it was no use. These medics were nosing around the kitchen all the time chasing down rumor the cooks had VD or TB or something. Waitresses were the subject of a good deal of speculation and innuendoes at Camp Canol at Norman Wells. In fact, as a practical joke somebody posted a list of their names and VD ratings on the bulletin board."

"I heard about that list," said Oscar. "Are you still mad at the medics for cutting off your raw milk?"

"That incident shows you how goofy these medics can get," spat Bob. "You see, fresh milk was one staple that was never available in our mess hall. But there was a farmer with a small herd of cows and he was selling milk to the boys for 50 cents a glass. It was quite an anomaly to see those big hard-bitten characters, used to brawling and scrapping, troop over to this farm just to get a glass of cool rich milk dipped from an earthenware crock. The demand was so great the farmer used to sell out in half an hour. That is, until the medics discovered the cows hadn't been tested for tuberculosis. There was almost a riot when the medics prohibited the farmer from selling raw milk to our men. But the bastards made it stick — and that ended the farmer's lucrative business."

Oscar admired young Canadians with the imagination to survive when working under adversity. Under adversity, the mess hall where Bob slaved provided good enough grub to get the navigation season off to a good start. The remaining freight for Canol was forwarded in ship-shape order.

The only fly in the ointment was the Americans had to bring in riverboat captains from the Missouri and Mississippi. They floundered around in strange waters, despite the fact Indians were brought in as pilots.

"These tough, devil-may-care captains didn't figure the Indians knew much," Matt Berry told Oscar when their paths crossed one day. "Some of them simply wouldn't believe Hudson's Bay pilots when they told them about being tied up two weeks at a time when 20-foot waves were kicked up. In the shallow waters, dangerous winds dumped tubs like rubber ducks."

"I heard there were a few notable sinkings that scared the hell out of them," said Oscar. "They never experienced such winds on the Mississippi," said Oscar.

"You're right, Oscar. Twenty diesel-operated refrigeration units of frozen beef ended up on a reef. Each camp along the Canol road was allocated one of these units. There was the possibility they wouldn't receive this ration, but in this case none went hungry. All but five tons were rescued. The U.S. Canuck Navy in Canada sent in an expert salvage crew which put small diesel units on each of the watertight refrigerators in the water. Until they could bring in barges to pick them up they remained there in good condition. I have to admire these Americans and their innovative minds in situations like this. They have another project at Fort Simpson of the same nature. Why don't you fly up there with me next week to see it?"

The following Thursday Oscar took off with Matt, who showed him that not all the freight was barged down the Mackenzie. A group of Swedes were busily engaged in cutting down lodgepole pines for $1 apiece and rafting them down the river for telephone poles.

"BPC is building a telephone line from Norman Wells along the Canol Road to Whitehorse," explained Matt. "In six months this will be the first land line that has ever connected the two towns."

Oscar was one of the few Canadians to ever use that phone line. He took the opportunity while in Ted Link's office in Norman Wells one day to take the receiver off a new phone there and tell "central" to put in a call "to Sverdrup and Parcel in Whitehorse, please."

He heard the phone ring and a female voice said, "Sverdrup and Parcel, Coleen Patterson speaking."

"Hello, this is Oscar. I've missed you so much."

"And I've missed you. But let's not tell everybody in the Northwest Territories. This is an open circuit party-line system. How are you? I received a big envelope in the mail today from your friend, George Midgeley of Tractor Train No. 42, with a copy of the log book for the rest of the trip after you retreated from the train at Axe Point. It's a valuable historical document. George detailed the grief, the break-downs and the difficulties. But when the train reached the Blackwater Lake rest stop, he waxed almost poetic about his experiences. I'll read it to you:

"The view across 12-mile-wide Blackwater Lake is beautiful. It reminded me more of home in Denver, Colorado than anywhere since I'd been in Canada. There was a range of snow-capped mountains across the lake that looked awfully big from the camp, but they were not likely over 4,000 feet high. The height made no difference to me. They were still the mountains I imagined I would be able to find over all the country instead of so much flatland with muskeg. The crew was never able to see much beyond the edge of the road as the trees were so thick. It makes a man feel lost when he can never see over the treetops. It is no wonder there are so many stories about getting bushed. Blackwater Lake was a grand place to relax before hitting that terrible road on the morrow."

"George is one of the good guys," Oscar agreed and then explained, "I had to call you, Coleen, to ask you a question that's been nagging me. Why haven't the bigwigs in Washington closed down the Canol Project? Is there some overarching reason you can think of for spending good money after bad?"

"Yes, dear Oscar, I think I may have an answer for you."

"OK, OK, come out with it. Don't keep me waiting."

"I'd tell you, but there may be big ears on this phone line. You have to come back to Whitehorse to see me. I'll take you home with me and whisper it in your ear."

"Cripes, can't you give me a ...?"

At that point the line went dead. Oscar rang again, but couldn't get Coleen back. He kept furrowing his brow and repeated over and over: "What's she know that I don't?"

VIII

It was late in 1943 when Oscar arrived back in Whitehorse for Coleen's birthday party. She looked like a bridesmaid waiting to catch a bouquet. But there was something else he couldn't put his finger on.

"What's this bantering look that you are walking around with all the time?" he demanded after the party. "What is it you know that I don't? Am I sleeping with the enemy? Or are you trying to tease me about my job? Or what, dammit?"

Her answer was all wrapped up in a big bear hug which shut off Oscar's serious thoughts.

Next day after work she met him at the Pig's Ear Bar ready to do some serious drinking. After a third daiquiri she brought a sheet of paper out of her purse. "This is one of these phony inter-office memos written by a couple of wiseacres. I hope you can see the satire in it without me having to draw you a picture. But there may be more wisdom than fiction. I'll read it to you, seeing I'm much more sober than you-all."

"Quote. *Memo to Dr. C.O.N. Buller, horse physician and surgeon and authority on everything: Locating a route for installation of Canol No. 1 was a job slated for six months, but was not completed for more than 18 months after the deadline set by the U.S. Army. In noting down the reasons why crews from both east and west were distracted from their mission, you may find complications which were byzantine. It is easy to lose the story line. If so, you may end up emulating the experience of the army and civilian engineers, the architects, experienced northern hands, greenhorns, surveyors, bush pilots, dog mushers, generals and working stiffs on the job.*

"In understanding the way the various crews criss-crossed the project, you have to stop and ponder, back up and start over, suffer boredom and repetition or take off on tangents to learn about the personalities involved and their adventures. Although this interdisciplinary group experienced delays, endured privations, had orders countermanded and fought among themselves, they may finally tame the elements. Nuts is

trump. Hail Hirohito. (Sgd) Dr. B.U.L. Conner, Horse Physician and Surgeon and Authority on Everything. Unquote."

"What's this commemorative footnote mean?" asked Oscar. "It says that this memo is dedicated to the suicide of A. Jones-McSmith, editor of the Canadian Good Roads Magazine. He tried to write a story on the construction of the Canol Road through the Mackenzie, Selwyn and Pelly Mountains. He pulled all his hair out first."

With that, he brought his fist down on the table so hard it scared everyone in the joint. "Now I see what you're trying to tell me. Goddamit. What a schemozzle this project is: The pipe and freight and the pump stations and personnel have been moved into Norman Wells and Whitehorse, but they've been held up waiting for somebody to give the construction crews a route location for putting it all together and in place! Is that what you're trying to tell me?" he shouted in 90-decibel disbelief.

"If you say so," replied Coleen sweetly, waiting for him to sound off some more, which he obligingly did. "I think this project should be abandoned. So does Senator Harry Truman of the Senate Investigating Committee. We have seen Lieutenant-Colonel Theodore Wyman, Jr. spending millions over-budget to ensure most of the frozen-in freight was delivered for an early start in this year's construction season and a route location for the road wasn't even completed by then. But they go on working despite being a year late. What gives?" he asked in frustration.

"I think I know, but I can't tell you in this bar. Let's go home."

Before Coleen could get her coat off, Oscar was at her with "What"s your theory?"

"Oscar, do you have a pencil?"

"Oh, a smartass?"

"Get it out then and do some quick arithmetic. Then you may have a clue why the Canol Project is kept going. Make a calculation about how many military people the United States has in the Canadian North and how many uniforms Canada has on site."

"Do I add or subtract?"

"It makes no difference." She giggled at his quizzical look.

Oscar shrugged indifferently and, after things cooled down, he asked Coleen where Guy Blanchet was flitting around these days. She didn't know for sure, but she would try to find out where the gritty little self-effacing Canadian land surveyor was. He was hired by J. Gordon Turnbull, the project engineer, to mastermind the route location.

"Blanchet is not the one to be seen sitting in a comfortable office sending out surveying crews. Like, he has been out there in the field him-self. He showed up around here in June to have a look at those mountains which had to be traversed. But there was so much uncertainty, infighting and fumbling, he was lost in the shuffle, so to speak," she said. "The rea-son Turnbull picked him was because after graduation from McGill University, the Ottawa-born Blanchet had worked as a prospector around Great Bear Lake. Then for 2½ years he was captain of a survey crew in the Canadian Army, but was invalided back to Victoria, British Columbia, with a heart attack. His doctor told him to get a desk job. But he was so serious about winning the war that, within a month, he had seconded him-self to the Canol Project."

"That almost gave his sawbones a heart attack I bet," said Oscar.

"Yes, he was flying around with Bud Potter doing an aerial recon-naissance for us to find an eastern access through those mountains. Bush pilots, white trappers and hunters avoided the mountains. Nobody else seemed to have the cold reserve to tackle the east end."

"Do you think Blanchet was the author of that letter circulated around Turnbull's office?"

Coleen gave him one of her eyes-averted sly looks and replied, "Maybe we'll never know."

"How do you know all this about Blanchet?" hounded Oscar.

"I met him when he reported to Turnbull. He kept a diary to which I was privy. I gathered from it that he had suffered a great deal of frustra-tion at the hands of the army engineers who thought civilian engineers were worms. He asked me to go flying with him. I couldn't get away, but reading his diary I know he pushed pilots to take too many risks with his demands. If I had gone up with him I'd likely have puked all over the plane."

"Ugh, what a way to go. But since you stayed on the ground you heard all about Blanchet's battles with the army brass from him."

"Yes," Coleen replied. "One of the epic battles of the Second World War is between Blanchet and Colonel Benjamin T. Rodgers of Buffalo, New York. Wait 'til I put on my war correspondent's hat and I'll tell you about it.

"It was almost a miracle that Blanchet, on his first flight with Bud Potter of the Canol Air Force, came up with a preliminary route out of Norman Wells that he later adopted as the permanent route."

"I heard an Indian guide, Paul Andrews of Fort Norman, told Blanchet about that route," put in Oscar.

"You're right. What actually happened was Blanchet took Paul up with him. Potter was opposed to using Indians as he contended they became confused and disoriented in a plane. And, indeed, this is what happened. Old Paul didn't know what Blanchet was really looking for; he thought he was looking for mountain goats for a hunting party. After a dog-fight with Potter, Potter turned the plane around and deplaned Paul, but not before Paul pointed out the magical route. Understand, Oscar?"

Oscar interjected: "But isn't it true Blanchet later discounted Paul's route as being too high. But later when he traversed the route by dog team, he discovered a different advantage. The Indian route led across the Carcajou River, up Dodo Canyon to a high plateau which was dubbed the Plains of Abraham. Although it traversed high peaks, it avoided the deep valleys on the way to Macmillan Pass."

"Who told you that?"

"My friend, Anton Money."

"Money evidently didn't know," she responded, "that Blanchet came up with a pioneer engineering trick of using the bed of a wide shallow river, the Carcajou, as a road up through Dodo Canyon. He knew this technique would work if some simple precautions were taken to guard against flash floods: the Carcajou had been known to rise 12 feet in 45 minutes; just send trucks through that danger spot in convoys.

"Blanchet didn't get back in June to do a traverse on foot to follow up his aerial reconnaissance. The foot traverse didn't happen until winter for two reasons. One was that Colonel Rodgers, the U.S. Army area engineer at Camp Canol, across the Mackenzie from Norman Wells, totally disregarded Blanchet's aerial work and attempted to build a road of his own choosing. The second was that Canol No. 1 was put on hold in June during the Japanese attack."

"What a bonehead Rodgers was," blurted Oscar. "Anton called him the Mad Colonel as he resented the presence of civilian engineers and surveyors on the job. The dumb cluck was scraping off overburden by the book, thus permafrost was giving him grief when it was uncovered and melted, and also his road was wandering into cul de sacs. Rodgers' trial roads were branching out from Camp Canol like a spider web. He lost dozens of bulldozers in that quagmire. By summer's end things had gone so badly that at one point serious consideration was being given to relocating the Canol No. 1 pipeline through Fairbanks. Only the intervention of General Somervell stopped that nonsense."

"I was there the day Somervell marched in and gave Turnbull the authority to tell the Mad Colonel to abandon 70 miles of road and proceed with the Indian route. But the Mad Colonel turned his big guns on Somervell and, wham, the army was without a road and Turnbull was on the spot. Turnbull's strategy was to form an alliance with Blanchet and together they routed Rodgers," Coleen sighed.

"I flew into Norman Wells and saw Rodgers' Palace on a promontory overlooking the Mackenzie Valley. How did he swing that?" asked Oscar.

"With $100,000 and peeled logs," chortled Coleen. "It had all the latest appointments and fixtures that could be brought in from the States. Nothing like it has ever been seen in the Northwest Territories. Of course, it could be argued, it is essential for entertaining prominent guests; he couldn't very well put them up in a tent." She went on to tell Oscar how Blanchet decided to travel the Indian route on foot. He had the reluctant connivance of Colonel Theodore H. Wyman, Jr., for this expedition. With a crew of seven Slavey Indians and 25 dogs, he mushed over the route, the first white man known to have done so.

"The fact that at night in camp the conversation was carried out in Slavey was how I came to get Blanchet's diary of this epic journey," said Coleen. "He couldn't understand Slavey so he had to find his own entertainment, which was writing a diary of a detailed account of the expedition and forwarding it to Turnbull's office. I just couldn't take my eyes off that little book. It was an epic of the North: crisp and to the point, but written by a man with the soul of a poet and determination of an explorer."

The perils of that 250-mile reconnaissance threatened to get Blanchet down: starvation, when the moose he expected to shoot for food weren't there, but lots of wolves were; exhaustion; and a severe injury to his foot. But he kept pressing on through the wild beauty of the subarctic land with names like the Sheep's Nest River, Fox Plains, Anthill Mountain, Egoche River, Itsi Mountains, Quiet Lake, Bluefish River, Godlin Lake, Tooritchie Mountain and Edele River. The beauty of the area of the eerie mountains and timber-filled plateaus offset the weariness and despair of breaking the long trail.

He and his crew finally reached Fred MacLennan's trading post at Sheldon Lake four days ahead of schedule on November 26. They all ate hearty for two days on food Blanchet had flown in to the post in advance. The Indians then went back with a copy of his notes for Turnbull in case anything happened to him.

"Why didn't he go back with the Indians?" pursued Oscar.

"It seems Turnbull had made a promise to send in a plane to pick him up when he arrived at MacLennan's. I thought you knew that."

"No, I hadn't heard that," said Oscar.

"Well, anyway, MacLennan was in a jackpot," Coleen went on. "His shortwave radio batteries had gone dead and a plane from Whitehorse scheduled to bring in groceries hadn't arrived due to bad weather. There was nothing Blanchet could do but wait, and wait and wait some more; a whole month and a half!"

"My God, this is one for the history books," he said.

"Blanchet's absence didn't concern Turnbull. Unbeknownst to Blanchet, Turnbull had despatched another route location party under Kent Fuller from Whitehorse to Sheldon Lake. Fuller was supposed to arrive at MacLennan's about the same time as Blanchet and a plane was ordered to pick both up. But Blanchet was not privy to this arrangement. Since MacLennan's radio had gone down he was kept in the dark, literally. It seems Fuller's party became a disaster and never did reach MacLennan's."

"This is another one for the books," marvelled Oscar. "What a cursory way to treat Blanchet."

"You may be interested in this note from his diary: *I was nearly driven over the edge in this solitary confinement. It was exacerbated when MacLennan ran out of coal oil for the lamps. We were in darkness in the 20-hour Arctic nights at this time of year. I spent many hours working out complicated mathematical formulas in my mind, spinning yarns of past adventures with MacLennan and plotting to keep George, the mink, an uninvited tenant, from constantly pulling my hair at night.*

"I was there the day Blanchet came barging into Turnbull's office with fire in his eye, forgetting about his heart attack, and heatedly demanding an explanation. Intimidated by an office full of military and civilian personnel intent on fighting a war, he got nowhere. The war now was not with the Japanese but with Senator Harry Truman's investigating committee bent on closing down the Canol Project. Back in civilization, Blanchet was only a small cipher in a juggernaut that had now been thrown into high gear. He was given no answers nor sympathy for his prolonged enforced stay in Sheldon Lake. Turnbull bustled him back to the Northwest Territories to do another reconnaissance project."

Oscar sent a copy of the Blanchet diary to Cecil (The Bull), his Washington master. He pictured his master's jaw dropping about a project so big that personnel were dropping out of sight for weeks. He was suitably flabbergasted at Blanchet putting himself in the hands of Phil Lucas of the Canol Air Force.

In a few days, Oscar was signalled by Senator Frank Jacobs for more hair-raising stories about the legendary Phil, the farmer turned bush pilot, to tell his friends around the U.S. capital. Oscar was only too pleased to tell Jacobs, "Most pilots aren't afraid of flying, but Phil's white-knuckle trips occurred only when he has Blanchet aboard looking for routes through the mountains.

"Blanchet simply has no fear in the air. Phil told me, 'He will take any risk in good or bad weather if I let him. He believes nothing can go wrong and the funny part of it is Blanchet is always right. He's talked me into so many tight spots I could qualify as a stunt pilot!' "

Coleen piped up, "I know Phil. He's my favorite bush pilot. He's a mild-mannered, matter-of-fact, lightly built character, and wonderful story-teller who looks like a teacher."

"Where'd you run into Phil?"

"He shows up at the office, tells the girls a bunch of yarns, then disappears. These stories about Blanchet mesmerize me. Like, he'd be up with Blanchet in the back seat with a pad on his knee taking notes in those unmapped mountains. When he didn't get all the details he'd order Phil to turn around and go back. He expected a pilot to make a U-turn in a canyon with 2,000 feet of rock walls. He'd get mad if the pilot pulled out to a safe turning place before going back. None of the other pilots said no to him, either, as he was too persistent and persuasive.

"Phil sits there calmly waving his arms in rolls and zooms to show us how Blanchet made him go to one side of a canyon and lay the plane up on the wing and come around again. He used to drive the pilots to drink."

"What a man. Jacobs will cherish that story," Oscar said.

"But there's more," said Coleen. "While Blanchet was in durance vile at Sheldon Lake, a new route location was ordered out of Camp Canol by J. Gordon Turnbull. Turnbull had received Blanchet's notes and, after studying them, lost no time ordering out the new party three days before Christmas, in 60-degree-below-zero weather. The unlucky leader was J.B. Porter, general manager of BPC. The party comprised 23 men, five bulldozers and cabooses. Your friends, Paul Andrews and Anton Money, were in that crew. Anton was there to provide 100 detailed gradient maps for the pipeline."

Oscar expressed curiosity: "Was it necessary to send in another party after Blanchet to do his work over?"

"No," she explained. "Blanchet had simply selected the most feasible location for a service road. Now gradient maps had to be drawn where the pipeline was to be built showing the elevations and distances between mountain passes in this previously unmapped territory. It was Anton's job to figure out whether oil could be pumped through the four-inch line at 1,200 pounds per square inch from Norman Wells to Whitehorse. It couldn't. It thus became necessary to install pumping stations about 50 miles apart. With this method, the whole system would not have to be shut down should the enemy bomb the line. Do you understand?"

"No, but you architects and engineers talk a different language."

"I'll give you some more data then. The pump stations had to be placed so the grade did not exceed $2\frac{1}{2}$% rise from the intake to the highest point. This means the topographical data from the field party had to be very accurate in determining the location of each pumping station."

"This is overkill," moaned Oscar. "All I want to know is will the oil flow at 60-below zero?"

"Yes," Coleen came back, "I just wanted to give you some basic engineering concepts. You should go to engineering school."

Oscar yawned.

"You still don't understand what I'm talking about, do you?" she demanded with some impatience.

"I think I'll stick to spying — but whatever is friction loss?" He yawned again as Coleen kept droning along about friction loss in Canol No. 1. He was more interested in the way the human element tackled those mountains in mid-winter. Anton Money supplied him with some of the adventures of the Porter party. Oscar unexpectedly ran into Anton trying to find some bourbon at the Pig's Ear Bar.

"Progress was slow as the terrain was treacherous, being filled with extraordinary sinkholes. I had never seen these before. We'd be following a stream for five or six miles, thinking this pass is wonderful, the grade is right and everything is going to work out splendidly. Then suddenly we'd come across a cirque, a precipitous mountain wall. There the creek would end in a sinkhole, going underground to God knows where. We had to retrace our steps and find another pass," said Money.

"Another event which slowed progress was that the Mad Colonel came along (after we had staked out the Indian road through Dodo Canyon) and tried to force us to follow the Gravel River route. There was a real battle this time and the field party went over the Mad Colonel's head to Edmonton and to Colonel Wyman. To make a long story short, the military in Edmonton came up and looked over the situation until we were right back to the Dodo Canyon route again.

"We kept slugging along until February 6, at which time we found ourselves out of food and out of radio contact. We decided to abandon the machines and return to Camp Canol."

As captivating as Anton's story about the temporary defeat and retreat from the elements by the Porter gradient survey party was, Coleen could find more dramatic reading in the Blanchet diary and his battle against the Mad Colonel.

"It's too bad the civilians couldn't find a way of having Colonel Rodgers court-martialed," said Oscar.

"You're not the first one to say that," she conceded. "But, yes, he was a bonehead. However, that wasn't the only occasion Blanchet and his route location forces had trouble with the military."

"And despite the fact it is now 2.30 a.m., pray tell about that."

Ignoring his inviting bedroom eyes, Coleen launched into the story of Blanchet's first reconnaissance assault to find a route on the west end of Canol No. 1 from Whitehorse to Sheldon Lake. Turnbull had sent him there after his reconnaissance on the east end of Canol No. 1 ended. The first 90 miles of the route were no problem as the pipe was laid alongside the Alaska Highway to Johnson's Crossing. The adventurous Bud Potter was at the controls of the plane as the route veered off from Johnson's Crossing into the bush through Ross River, a trading post at the junction of the Pelly and Ross Rivers, on to Sheldon Lake.

When Blanchet submitted his summer aerial reconnaissance notes to J. Gordon Turnbull, Turnbull was able to commandeer a U.S. Army survey party from Alaska Highway construction work and had them sent on a ground survey from Johnson's Crossing to Ross River.

"Turnbull was pretty tickled at this coup and also at securing the services of the 93rd and 35th Engineering Regiments to follow up by building a winter road," said Coleen.

"He was much less exuberant when word reached him that upon reaching Quiet Lake, 45 miles east of Ross River, the army surveyors walked off the job after reporting to Edmonton it was impossible to build a road or pipeline through this country," reported Coleen. "Turnbull solved this dilemma by sending out a survey party headed by Kent Fuller; you know, the surveyor who was supposed to meet Blanchet at Sheldon Lake, but didn't make it. Fuller discovered the army surveyors had gone wrong in failing to move caches of food and supplies ahead of them over the river system and then work both ways from the caches. Ironically, the stretch from Johnson's Crossing to Quiet Lake, where the army had given up, was the worst part of the whole route to locate. Had they persevered a bit longer they would have been all right.

"With the onset of an early winter, Fuller saw tractor trains were going nowhere fast, so he decided to use seven pack horses. He had forgotten horses eat hay and oats, thus making it mandatory to organize an aerial haylift from Carcross via George Simmons' Northern Airways. No grass grows on the rocks and muskeg in this area of the Yukon."

"Gee, what an operation this must have been," commented Oscar. "What yarns the pilots must have been able to tell in the bar about running a taxi service convertible into a flying hay wagon."

"Us people around Sverdrup and Parcel will be talking about an air drop of hay to horses on the Canol Project for 100 years," laughed Coleen. "Those poor horses became casualties. They proved useless when the party encountered snow drifts 10 to 15 feet deep in November. Fuller had to revert to bringing in Indians with dog sleds from Ross River. The horses were shot to provide feed for the dogs. The Indians stayed with the Fuller party which was running stadia survey lines to Sheldon Lake. Even the most seasoned Northerner can never prepare for the eventualities of the trail, it seems. When the party reached a forward food cache, they found the squirrels had destroyed all the food but the flour. They only survived by eating flour mixed with muskrat meat for a week."

"By golly, old Cecil (The Bull) will be eating up these stories and wanting to know how much this hay cost," said an awed Oscar.

Next spring Turnbull brought in 188 more horses and Blanchet. Blanchet was sent out to cope with delays which had bogged things down for weeks at a time due to heavy rains which fell most of the summer. The surveyors used the horses to make detailed route surveys for BPC crews building the permanent Canol No. 1 road. The haylift was carried out by Pat Callison, a Peace River bush pilot, with Northern Airways.

"He used to show up at the office and tell us about winning the war singlehandedly flying hay in for those damned horses for five months," Coleen revealed.

"And who grew the hay in the Yukon?" asked a curious Oscar.

"Oh, that was no problem. The best hay and oats that the army could find in the United States were shipped in by boat to Skagway right under the noses of the Japanese Navy. In addition to the hay, Callison flew out rations for 28 horse wranglers, 28 surveyors and some Indian guides."

"That must have been the most expensive hay in history."

"It was. George Simmons and his fleet of three bush planes logged 150,000 hours on the hay plus other contracts he had with the U.S. Army. He was paid $85 an hour against costs of $28. Although Callison and the pilots made many forced landings, the operation was carried out without an injury."

And so to bed. When Oscar woke up in the morning he told Coleen about the funniest dream he ever had: some bush pilots were throwing horses out of their planes down to bales of hay on the ground. "How could this be?" he asked groggily.

"Hah, hah. You idiot. It was the other way around," said Coleen in gales of laughter.

"I don't believe that, either," mumbled Oscar.

"Well, here it is in Blanchet's diary. Read all about it there."

J. Gordon Turnbull's survey teams and BPC's road crews under J.R. Wells on the west end of Canol No. 1 were having as bad a time in wet weather. They came to a standstill. Turnbull finally solved the problem by beefing up Fuller's crews and pushing them east of Sheldon Lake to fast-track Wells and Company out of the mud.

The survey was completed in September, when the two crews met at Anthiel River, 90 miles east of Norman Wells, after working through the high rugged country with its castellated peaks, high passes and August snow storms.

"I thought Callison and his buddies would be finished flying in those mountains in September, but the army kept them and the Canol Air Force on standby until February," Coleen told Oscar. "That's when the welders installed the last joint of pipe. The road builders had finished in December."

"I'd like to meet this character, Callison," Oscar said. "He might have a good story that will titillate Cecil (The Bull)."

"That can be arranged this afternoon as I am sure he will be in the office. When he comes in with his stories about flying on one wing, everything stops and they all cheer, especially us girls."

Oscar showed up when the ebullient Callison was at the centre of attention with a story about a pilot everyone knew as the "Ribstone Rustler," who was asked to fly a rubber tire seven feet in diameter off Teslin Lake on the Alaska Highway to a dirt moving machine at Ross River.

"He couldn't get it into the cabin of the little Fairchild, so he followed standard bush pilot procedure and lashed it to the spreader bar of the floats.

But when he had left the lake he saw the huge tire had filled with water from the spray of the floats. This not only bogged down the plane, but, worse still, it threw water at the plane's engine. The engine began to miss. Not being sure what the problem was, the Ribstone Rustler shut her down and taxied back to the dock and unloaded the tire," recounted Callison.

"Unable to figure out what was making the engine miss, he decided to go back to home base at Carcross and have it checked out. He took off and climbed just high enough to make sure of doing an emergency landing if the engine quit. The engine was fine until he landed on Bennett Lake, then it cut out completely. A boat came out and towed the Ribstone Rustler and the plane to the dock. When the mechanic, B.B.Q. Bouffioux, opened the lid he discovered a chunk about the size of a 25-cent piece had fallen out of the intake pipe, which had caused the manifold to lose pressure. It must have been hanging on by a thread, so to speak, and, when he throttled back after landing, it fell out. Losing all the manifold pressure, the engine stopped dead. The cold water spraying onto the hot pipe had cracked it. After repairs were made, the Rustler went coolly back and delivered the tire. This time, though, he lashed it to the side of the plane. Gad, what a man."

Callison stopped to say hello to Coleen and Oscar on the way out. He indicated his job was over on the project and he was going back to a civilian job.

"Ever thought of getting a job hauling some of that 'special' cargo out of Port Radium on Great Bear Lake?" Oscar asked him innocently. Callison's answer was to grab him by the throat and stand him against the wall nose-to-nose. In a hard cold voice he demanded, "How do you know about that?"

"Hey, take it easy," squirmed Oscar. "Don't you know we have a phone line in this country now?"

"Lookit here, kid, just forget about these hush-hush flights. The pilots doing the flights have been told if they open their traps about what they are carrying, they'll be court-martialed by the U.S. Army. Button your lip."

Oscar was wise enough to take a hint, but he promised himself to hustle over to Port Radium later to see what he could find out. That would be after the grand official opening and big drunk at the Whitehorse oil refinery in a couple of weeks and some of the dignitaries might have a clue.

Coupled with the big secret Coleen had been hinting at, he finally figured out she might be on to something big — and not only hush-hush, but top secret and horrific. He was surprised that she was not indignant at the way Callison had handled him, but he decided to hold his peace. Cecil (The Bull) was mighty interested, but told him to be careful.

The day before Oscar had finally cleared the decks for the trip to Port Radium to finally find out what the mysterious shipments were about, he had a call over the new phone line that had been built from Edmonton to Fairbanks by the U.S. Signal Corps. It was from Cecil (The Bull): "I hear there's a press tour of the Alaska Highway and the Canol Project going through Whitehorse next week. Why don't you get yourself certified to travel with this bus full of drunks — excuse me, reporters — and see if they know anything about these mysterious shipments out of Port Radium? I'll approve extra expenses for you to prime them with more overproof rum. See what they know after a few drinks."

Coleen was surprised — and pleased — that he had more time around Whitehorse to stay with her. She offered to show him a few American tricks for winning poker games.

"I doubt if you'll drink any of them under the table," she added with a straight face. "You haven't done it to me yet."

"But one of them is more likely to tell me the big secret — which you won't tell me," he whispered.

She again gave him that knowing smile of hers.

IX

Leaving Coleen's cellblock in Whitehorse a couple of days later, Oscar set out on a historic mission which turned into a hysterical junket. It was the inauguration of scheduled Greyhound bus service over the Alaska Highway and Canol Project between Dawson Creek and Fairbanks. Later, as a propaganda effort, the U.S. Army had organized a 1,525-mile press tour. Oscar had been alerted to this tour by Cecil (The Bull) and was told to join it in Whitehorse. In preparation, he had taken a short course from Coleen on how to win at U.S.-style poker.

"There's going to be 60 newsmen on this trip, all of whom play poker and all of whom are accomplished cheats," she said brightly. "Now I've taught you their game, you can go and beat them at their own game and take all their money."

"Right you are, Coleen. In my travels I have become quite convinced Yankees are compulsive gamblers who will bet on anything living or dead any time, day or night."

"Once you see Colonel Patsy O'Connor and get yourself accredited as a reporter for the Picture Butte Bugle, you may be able to sneak in a few questions which Cecil (The Bull) is itching to have answered. You may even hear some of the gossip I have encountered about why the military is keeping the Canol Project alive when it should be dead." This was followed by another of her enigmatic grins.

One of Oscar's abiding memories of his entire association with the Yanks was that when there was a lull in work activity they would break out a pair of dice or a poker deck. In their time off, most of them would invariably head for the barracks or a club (in locations where such a luxury was available) to sit in on one of the wide open poker games that ran 24 hours a day.

A few days after pay day it was common to see the resident "scientist" sending home a money order for more than $1,000, having "discovered" all the loose money in camp. Most of the Yanks Oscar knew didn't waste time in "little league" games. Most were in a hurry to get into action games like ace-away, jingalo or four-five-six.

Officially, the army and civilian brass frowned on high-rolling sharks because their activities often resulted in fights. The camps housed many Texans and Oklahomans on the projects. The Oklahomans didn't hesitate to pull a knife to settle affairs of honor. The Texans carried guns.

"The biggest game I knew about was in the camp atop the hill in Whitehorse. Alfie Bryan told me one of the most memorable games started the night a bus driver for BPC called Dutch got real hot. Over the next couple of days he and his partner, Tex Nichols, cleaned the boys out of $24,000," said Oscar. "Alfie told me he decided to go after a piece of the action, but after dropping $200 he got out and stood back to watch Dutch clean out 150 more guys. The pair simply lined them up and took their wallets. When the money ran out the losers paid with shirts, watches, hats. Word soon spread around town and two different gangs showed up to take a crack at the pot, but Dutch cleaned them out, too. Then Dutch began drinking a bottle of rum he had won. He became so drunk he could hardly stand, but he kept right on winning."

"I never heard the complete story of that wild night," said Coleen. "But I did hear that when it came time for the Dutch-Tex partnership to divide their winnings 50/50 a few days later there was a terrible scene. Dutch's mind was still inflamed with demon rum. He mumbled drunkenly that he had done all the work so Tex was only entitled to 10 per cent, or $2,400."

"That is only part of the story," explained Oscar. "Tex went for his knife and slashed Dutch across the stomach. Letting out a great roar, Dutch picked up the six-foot Tex and threw him through the flimsy barrack door. Alfie and others standing near Dutch saw that the strain on his wound caused his stomach to rupture and his guts came spilling out. Alfie gathered him up and I dusted off his intestines a bit, stuffed them back in and ran for the doctor. There wasn't much blood, but there sure were a lot of guts. I never did learn how they finally split up the money, but I saw Dutch limping around three weeks later and he was broke. In addition to his knife wounds, he also suffered from a disease common to all chronic gamblers. He'd gone back to a game and got cleaned out."

"What happened to Tex? Did he go crazy?" Coleen asked.

"Alfie stepped into the breach with some more of us, but it was Toughie Griffiths, a mail truck driver for Metcalfe-Hamilton Kansas City Bridge and former boxer and alley fighter, who finally subdued him.

The RCMP came and placed him under arrest — in their barracks. Sentenced to a month in this durance vile, Tex was required to rake leaves and attend flowers. He performed his gardening duties flawlessly and behaved so well they gave him a week off his sentence."

"So Toughie was in the Tex-Dutch squabble, too?" interposed Coleen. "He was one and the same who gained some notoriety with a knife a few weeks later when he returned to the MHKCB dormitory to find another man in bed with his live-in girlfriend. Grabbing the guy, Toughie dragged him outside the dormitory and castrated him. A number of terrified women watched as the guy bled to death. Fortunately for Toughie, his employers had enough pull with the law to convince the authorities that the aggrieved Toughie was performing an essential job and should not be held in custody. In a camp where there were 10 men for every woman, the code of 1943 rough northern frontier justice prevailed: it was open season on any man who laid hands on another's woman. Toughie's action was deemed 'lawful' and he went back to work to help win the war."

The only thing that eclipsed the American penchant for excitement at Whitehorse was the arrival of those big blue Greyhound buses carrying the newsmen on tour. Coleen, seeing the bus, thought she was experiencing a mirage. She had seen Greyhounds daily in Kansas City, but hadn't seen one for two years in Whitehorse. Her awe was only exceeded by the natives who had never seen a Greyhound previously. Bringing this rudiment of civilization into the virgin bush of the Yukon, much of which was unexplored territory two years ago, impressed both Yanks and natives more than any other wartime accomplishment.

Greyhound made capital of the accomplishment by advertising: "Greyhound can run buses anywhere the U.S. Army can build roads. Tokyo, here we come!"

It was with great anticipation that the case-hardened Oscar lugged his duffelbag aboard a Greyhound for his first trip to the United States (Alaskan territory). He was the only passenger who kissed his girlfriend goodbye at the temporary bus terminal in Whitehorse. There was a cheer from the assemblage as he took a seat. Most of the newsmen had hangovers from a big shindig the night before. The army had put them up at the overwhelmingly large army base with its officers' mess, monstrous bar and private rooms. The officers of the Northwest Service Command were glad to have company from stateside as they were "bushed" in the Yukon.

Oscar reached the sad conclusion after the first 150 miles into the trip that he wasn't going to pump any eye-popping secrets of Canol No. 1 from any of the boys. He shared a seat with Eldon Stonehenge of the Toronto Globe and he asked Eldon what the army tour leaders had told the group about the Canol Project. The buses had travelled along the pipeline which had been laid beside the Alaska Highway 85 miles from Johnson's Crossing to Whitehorse.

"The Canol Project? What's that?" Eldon asked with a puzzled look.

"Didn't you see that pipeline running alongside the highway?" countered Oscar.

"Well, yes, we did, but nobody from the army said a word about the pipeline being part of the highway project. You mean to tell me the army is going to pump oil 625 miles through a small pipe like that?" shouted Eldon.

Instantly Oscar became the centre of attention for a dozen others as they prodded him for more details. He obligingly supplied them.

His "scoop" ended quietly and quickly 10 minutes later when a big uniform marched down the length of the bus and said in a loud voice: "You guys have never heard a thing the kid has told you nor have you seen that pipeline. Any more discussion and you'll all be off this tour before a court-martial."

That was it. There were knowing glances — and a deathly silence. Oscar hunkered down in his seat. In his stream of consciousness he began to see acres of braid on a huge number of U.S. Army personnel. Coleen drifted into the picture with the observation, "And there weren't any Canadian uniforms in sight?"

He replied "no."

With that peculiar look in her eye again she drove home, "Now you're catching on fast to my secret."

When the buses reached Beaver Creek, the border-crossing point into Alaska, the friendliness of the officers' mess changed to hard-nosed security. All passengers were required to be fingerprinted. Then the diesel-powered electrical plant failed at the customs office, leaving the five men on duty processing those on board by flashlight.

Oscar was left in a fit of laughter when he next contacted Cecil (The Bull): "Those U.S. Immigration yokels didn't know what to do with us Canadians — us Canadians who are allowing you Yanks to clutter up our landscape like incurable eczema. They took a look at Bill Stavdal of the Calgary Stampeder and Moses O'Hara of the Edmington Bulletin and weren't going to allow them into the United States because they looked like subversives as they had no U.S. passports. The escorting officers from the U.S. Army were called in to explain their presence. They came and pulled rank on the Immigration blokes and told them to smarten up when dealing with good neighbors and to 'stuff' their regulations.

"When I came before one of the flat-faces with a flashlight, he demanded to know where I came from. I replied 'Alberta.' His response was 'what state is that in?' I tried to explain to this kid from Tennessee that Alberta is a province in Canada and Picture Butte is a little burg in that province. He immediately issued me with a pass reading 'Littleburg, Alberta.' That pass followed me everywhere I went in Alaska," Oscar reported to Cecil (The Bull).

The hosts gave the tour members a four-day leave in Fairbanks. The buses left for other duties and the army laid on planes to fly them out.

Coleen's reaction to Oscar's marginal notes on the Fairbanks locals was, "You sound almost libelous in describing them as a colorful assortment of bootleggers, gamblers, prostitutes and characters. Fairbanks booze is rotgut.

"There was nothing for the newsmen to do but organize a marathon revolving crap game. By Day Four most of the fellows had enough of gambling as most were broke and were ready to go home," said Oscar. He discovered as hard as Yanks fought over their "games," Canadians were just as vehement. He saw a show of deep-seated animosity between Allen Bill of the Calgary Herald and Hal Straight of the Vancouver Sun break out when a verbal agreement dissolved into a raging dispute. The two editors grabbed each other's throats. In no time every stick of furniture was smashed by the weight of these two hefty sworn enemies.

An ashen-faced Oscar recalled that "With great personal courage, the army personnel in charge of a war-within-a-war managed to restore calm and get the game rolling again. The first bet had just been made when some trucks arrived from Ladd Field to pick us up for the flight home. There came a knock on the door and a driver said, 'The colonel says your plan is leaving in two hours.'

" 'Tell the colonel to hang tough,' came back a drunken reply. 'We're still playing poker.' "

Inexplicably, despite the fact planes were scarce, this scene was played out time after time. Unbelievably, public relations took precedence over bad manners and that plane was held there for two days. Oscar's friend, Major Eugene Kush of army public relations, was awarded a purple heart for cleaning up this imbroglio.

"Responding to an attack of conscientiousness, one reporter decided he should make an appearance at the airport. Unable to continue to countenance continued delay, the pilot took off with one passenger. This affair created a helluva schmozzle as it meant that about 60 men were stranded and now they had to find their own way home," Oscar reported to Cecil (The Bull). "Among the many suggestions put forward, Allen Bill put in a call to Prime Minister Mackenzie King. Some of the others called Washington, but their bravery in doing so ran out. Luckily, I happened to know my way around the military by then and hitched a ride on the daily mail plane," Oscar confessed to Coleen when he stumbled into her cellblock.

She greeted Oscar with mock seriousness and pointed out the press tour escapade was the talk of the town "and aren't you people ashamed of yourselves. By the way, how much money did you win?"

"Jealousy will never get you anywhere," was all Oscar could think of to say.

"Well, then, what did you find out from that bunch of gossip-mongers?"

"I'm sorry to say they know nothing from nothing. They were simply overwhelmed by the world-class scope of this top-secret project. They were open-mouthed; asking me questions. But I found you two pair of nylons in Fairbanks that hadn't been scooped up by those Russian women pilots who were coming there to pick up American fighter planes and ferrying them back to the Stalingrad front."

Once the Canol Project was in operation and there was less Japanese pressure on them, American military officers organized "fun tours" for visiting dignitaries along the 625-mile road. Oscar happened to be in the right place at the right time to be invited by Brigadier-General F.S. Strong, commanding officer of the Northwest Service Command, to go on one of the junkets.

"I wish you could come, too, and see the results of your handiwork," Oscar told Coleen. "But Strong told me to come and bring my Speed Graphic. That means I will only be able to bring you some pictures; also some for Cecil (The Bull) to satisfy his curiosity and show him I was not feeding him a myth for the last two years."

"Who else is along for the fun this time?"

"There's Air Vice Marshal T.A. Lawrence of the Northwest Staging Route and Brigadier-General D.V. Gaffney, head of the Alaskan Wing of the U.S. Army Air Force."

"You'll have to be on your best behaviour with all that brass on hand."

"I'll tell you all about it if I don't freeze in this 65-below weather."

Oscar was amazed at the fleet of vehicles Strong had organized for the mid-winter safari: five double-heated staff cars, two ambulances, two doctors and a carry-all van for the luggage.

"It was fascinating to travel the Canol Road now that it was finished and oil was running through the pipeline. In the Mackenzie Mountains the tree cover ran out at 4,000 feet, making the terrain bleak and barren. On the fourth day we entered the old Peele River Game Preserve where big signs were posted advising that only natives could shoot as they needed big game for subsistence," Oscar related.

"Travelling along a high mountain road we came to an alpine meadow where our sudden approach disturbed more than 300 ptarmigan in full winter dress that was as white as the snow on which they were sitting eating willow buds. All the Americans had firearms of one kind or another. Despite the signs, they stopped to break out their M-1s and started potting away at the birds.

"The ptarmigans were very tame and didn't even fly when the artillery opened up. They were hard to see against the snow, but finally Gaffney managed to knock over two. He went waddling off the road in four feet of snow for about 150 feet to pick up those two damned birds and held them up for us all to see.

"At this point we had travelled for four days without seeing any traffic. However, just at the moment Gaffney triumphantly held up those birds, a jeep rounded a bend in the road with two RCMP sergeants. You'd almost have thought they had been waiting for him to do it. They stopped and Gaffney came back to the car with those things tucked behind his back like a kid with his hand in the cookie jar. The RCMP kept him standing there at 40-below chatting about the weather, the trip and miscellany for 15 minutes. Gaffney was almost petrified by the cold."

In the meantime, Lieutenant Nemesis P. Goosehabit, Gaffney's aide, came running back, scared stiff, to Oscar. He had a gun as well as that funny Hungarian name, thrust it at Oscar to put under the seat in the staff car and said, "Don't say a word about this gun."

"What in hell are you talking about?" asked a puzzled Oscar.

"Those are RCMP and this is a game preserve."

"Oh, for God's sake. They won't say anything to a couple of guys shooting ptarmigan. They're just making sure nobody is cleaning out the game preserve," Oscar remonstrated.

"Well, you don't know these Mounties," Nemesis P. Goosehabit whispered. "They're tough. So don't say a word."

When the party arrived at the next camp, Gaffney gave his ptarmigan to the cook and asked him to serve them for breakfast. Then he consulted with another member of the touring group, Major-General W.W. Foster, who was a special Canadian commissioner for northwest defence projects. He had been former chief of police in Vancouver. Oscar overheard what happened next to this decorated officer who was almost overcome with apoplexy. "Look, you're an old policeman and I'm in a bit of trouble."

"Oh," said Foster.

"Yes. I was shooting a few ptarmigan up on top this afternoon and a couple of Mounties came along while I was doing it. What do you think will happen?"

"Oh, my dear fellow, nothing will happen. I know that's a game preserve, but it isn't aimed at distinguished American officers who want to have some sport on a winter afternoon. Of course, you understand they'll have to charge you as a matter of form," Foster said with a straight face.

"Prosecute me?" Gaffney yelped, turning a shade whiter.

"Oh, yes," said Foster. "They have no choice about issuing a summons. They'll make it easier for you, though. They can change the venue to Edmonton."

"What do you mean? Appear in court?"

"You'll have to appear and they'll give you a chance to plead guilty. But the magistrate is a friend of mine. I'll have a word with him. I don't think it will cost you more than a couple of hundred dollars."

"I could just imagine what was going on in Gaffney's head: court martial, cashier, sent home in disgrace for muddying up Canada-U.S. relations and God knows what else. Worse still, his name might be in the papers," Oscar reminisced to Coleen later. "Nemesis P. Goosehabit arranged for the Mounties to get to the overnight camp before the boss arrived and tip them off to his plight. Foster kept Gaffney, defender of America, in utter agony for the next couple of days, then his aide finally tipped him off they were pulling his leg."

With a wrinkled brow, she said, "About this Nemesis P. Goosehabit. What does the 'P' stand for?"

"Ptarmigan," and there was a loud guffaw. Gaining her composure, Coleen coaxed, "I suppose after he had eaten the birds and had a few drinks, he could finally relax."

"Oh, yes! The gourmet food he laid on for this trip was more spectacular than the scenery: out of this world. Golly, this wonderful food caused me an embarrassment almost as great as Gaffney's gaffe. I recall bacon, cream, canned fruit, T-bones, butter, egg souffles, baked Alaska and Arctic char. But the food was even better at a big banquet at the Norman Wells Hotel at the end of the trip. After a huge turkey, I said to Vice-Admiral Lawrence, 'God, I can't eat all this.' 'Oscar,' he told me, 'you're going to eat it and like it, too.' Bursting at the seams I did manage some pickled beets and jellied fruit salad."

Oscar teased Cecil (The Bull) about the gourmet dishes on the Canol safari for weeks. He could hear him drooling and "damning those sons of bitches up there living off the fat of the land and I haven't bitten into a T-bone for more than a year. I'm going to get Gaffney cashiered for this," and he hung up in a fury.

Sharing his notes with Coleen pleased Oscar very much, especially when she enthused, "Oscar, you are one of the few Canadians ever to have travelled over this project while it was still producing gasoline. You have a story here that is a historic masterpiece."

"I suppose you are right. I never thought of it that way until you brought it up. Your insight is terrific." He was silent for a while. He was about to say something, but he hesitated. "Yes?" she questioned. "Coleen, have you ever been in New York?"

"Only once when I was a teenager. What makes you ask something like that out of the blue?"

"I overheard some the brass talking a couple of times about Manhattan; like Manhattan in Chicago. That sounded kind of funny because I know Manhattan is in New York."

"You're right, it is in New York. What else were they saying about Manhattan?"

"Nothing that seemed to make any sense to me. They were saying it was top secret and something about Manhattan was going to end the war — and that would end those plane flights out of Port Radium. And things like that that sounded weird."

Coleen sat for a long time in silent contemplation, then spoke up: "You will recall that I asked you why this over-budget Canol Project has been kept going so long and why are there more U.S. Army personnel here than Canadian Army types, as you noted in the officers' mess that night?"

"Yes, but what's that got to do with Manhattan?"

"Manhattan is the code name for a U.S. Army project. But it will take me a long time to tell you what I have found out about it. Let's get some sleep and I'll tell you my theory tomorrow. And, Oscar, do you think you and I could make a trip into the Eldorado mine at Port Radium some time?"

He gave "maybe" and a shrug for an answer and wondered if she had been suffering from delusions or cabin fever. And so to bed with a lover who could always surprise him.

With Coleen's promise of a morning surprise, sleep that night came quickly. Her strong, languorous legs entwined with his wafted him into a dream that was exotic or erotic, but not necessarily in that order. The exotic reverie took him back to that Greyhound bus trip with that group of hard-boiled poker sharks drinking free booze while the slobs at Canadian Press in Hogtown were suffering alcoholic withdrawal syndrome due to wartime booze rationing and turned down his series of stories on the commencement of the Alaska Highway. His vindictive laughter woke them both up. When he got back to sleep again he had an erotic dream about discovering a weekly newspaper editor at Fort St. John, British Columbia, who took a liking to him the minute he entered her sanctum sanctorum.

Maggie McMurphyvisk was a salty-tongued, fire-eating, hard-drinking, feisty, well-endowed woman whose syntax-mangled stories reflected her tongue. Many of the editions of her Alaska Highway Views became collector's items on this account.

"I was born in 1888 in Kansas and still keep my American citizenship," Maggie pointed out. "I came to Vancouver and went to work on a small paper run by a handsome, loving country editor with a shirttail full of type and a Country Campbell press — and I married all three of them. I helped George start two other newspapers at Squamish and Lillooet, British Columbia. And I stood by him until he achieved his career wish of being elected a member of Parliament to become a champion of the Canadian Northwest. Now he's away from home too much for my liking fighting this war."

"And here you are doing the same thing as me," added Oscar. "Only while I am filing reports across the border to the FBI about what your Yankee compatriots are doing on this project, you are filing front-page stories on American GIs in the Chicago Tribune."

"That's for damshur," she said in a phrase that became her trademark all over the North. "And so you want to know how I ever landed in this raw pioneer town. Well that's easy. I declared war on the Japs four years before the United States did."

"Oh, quit that Irish blarney of yours, Maggie," teased Oscar.

"I really developed an indelible hatred of them after George and I were in Shanghai on a Canadian government mission and the Japs bombed the city: a horrifying experience. Then when Canada declared war on them, the government shipped the Japs inland from the coast and one of these internment camps was set up at Lillooet where I was editing the weekly paper. I decided I would never live in the same town as them. I made a trip to Fort St. John and figured this whirlwind of U.S. activity would result in a thriving town for a weekly paper. And here I am. We closed down the Squamish paper and transferred the rationed newsprint quota to this paper in Fort St. John."

"Besides those stories on all the plane crashes I see you write every week, you are hammering hell out of your compatriots from stateside for all the 'legal waste,' as you call it."

"That's for damshur, too. I blew the whistle on this waste because I'm damshur outraged by it. Look here, goddamit, you come over to the house and I'll cook you a moose steak and tell you what 'they' are doing to me."

Walking up to Maggie's door that night, Oscar knocked and opened it and put in his arm with a pair of nylons in his hand. He was greeting with a scream of delight and Maggie yelling, "I don't care who you are, but if you have nylons, come on in. I miss stockings more than I do George."

She gave him a heart-stopping hug, a fine steak — it was the first time he'd ever had moose — and a stiff drink of rum to put him in the mood for listening to her sensual and loud invective on waste. She had been brought up on the pioneering credo that "wastefulness is sinful."

"We are trying to get a hospital going here. Supplies are scarce. So is badly needed equipment; and pharmaceuticals and every other damn thing like mattresses, beds, sheets and chairs. The American forces have all these things in surplus. But as they prepare to withdraw from the projects they are trashing many of the things we are begging for: burning them or throwing them over the banks of the Peace River. Six hundred pounds of sugar, which is rationed in Canada, went to the dump. I get so bloody mad when they try to tell me their rationale for these wanton actions. They say their agreement with Canada is that anything they can't use must be sent back home. The Canadian government says it doesn't want any of their surplus to go on the market and put Canadian businessmen out of business."

Nevertheless, agreement or not, it made hard-pressed and war-weary Canadians weep in anguish to see wholesale lots of scarce food buried in dumps and hard goods like engines (which can't be bought in Canada) smashed beyond repair. So the press took up the cry of "immoral, legalized" waste.

"I saw some of your impassioned editorials. But the poor GIs and camp foremen were under orders and they ignored your piteous pleas," Oscar informed her.

"That was until I resorted to a well-known ploy of weekly editors and called up Bob Beattie of the Vancouver Province and gave him a ready-made scoop. His story about the waste went across Canada on the Canadian Press wire. There was a great deal of indignation that this was going on at a time when the United Nations Relief and Rehabilitation Administration was soliciting people to save their old clothes for the destitute in Europe while new stuff in Fort St. John was being burned. Some changes are being made to halt the destruction, but much of the damage has been done."

The Americans hid behind their articles of war policy in which unused articles were classified as waste and this allowed them to write everything off.

"What was the official reaction to Beattie's exposé in the Vancouver Province?"

"Hah, we simply got a lot of government denials of waste and fraud. What else could the government say? But denials, which we had seen with our own eyes, did not hurt us as much as the efforts of the army brass to cover up the situation with all those bloody unctuous lies."

"You gave Beattie some follow-up stories?"

"That's for damshur. And it wasn't until after I said it in an editorial in the Alaska Highway Views that no investigation was thought necessary of the people who participated in wasteful procedures or the taxpayers who were victims of them. That brought the FBI and the RCMP in on the double. But I thought their investigation was wishy-washy."

"And I suppose you were thwarted by newspaper censorship and military secrecy which was used to silence the critics, as were a few truckloads of scarce goods which were dropped off at strategic locations," Oscar offered.

"The only comeback I could think of: 'I expect when the story of this wartime project is told by the historians that the waste will be justified — waste which we are told does not exist.' I was never so mad as the time at the end of the construction season when thousands of badly needed sleeping bags and wool blankets were taken to an army laundry and cleaned. Then all were taken away and burned. They evidently didn't want to have a dirty fire so they had to clean the stuff first. It burned me up."

"That's for damshur," said Oscar. And they both laughed delightedly that he had picked up on her trademark. He went back to an army bunk-shack, hit the sack — and dreamed about Maggie.

The next time he was in the sack he woke up 4 a.m. cussing and swearing. His language was much to the consternation of Coleen.

"Whatever are you talking about?" asked a sleepy Coleen.

"I dreamed the Americans were going to walk away and abandon the Alaska Highway and Canol Project and cede them to the Canadian government. But the Canadian government thought the whole thing was an expensive pile of junk and was going to abandon them, too. However, Maggie and other editors in the North reacted with horror and forced Ottawa to reverse its decision."

"Who's Maggie?" demanded Coleen.

"A friend of mine in Fort St. John. She told me how her husband got up in the House of Commons and persuaded the government to designate the Canadian Army and the War Assets Corporation to take possession and set up a Canadian-American team to value the contents, then arranged to pay 10 cents on the dollar for them."

"You're dreaming," scoffed Coleen.

"No, Maggie went on to tell me how furious she was about what that team found."

"Yeh, what?" asked Coleen with an edge to her voice.

"Well, they found 3,500 mattresses in one warehouse, two boxcars of circular dining room tables at McCrae, a monstrous dump of oil and gasoline at Burwash Landing, two dozen female breast pumps at an oil pumping station on Canol No. 1 and 1,200 gravel trucks with all the carburetors smashed.

"How do you like the way tax dollars were pissed away? Another outrageous act occurred at Watson Lake. Despite the fact there were coal deposits everywhere along the Alaska Highway, the Americans hauled 350,000 tons into Dawson Creek from Seattle. Hundreds of tons were then trucked to Watson Lake. It was not all used, whereupon it was dumped over the brow of a hill and covered with dirt. Reverend Michael Schmidt found the mine and supplied his Roman Catholic parishioners with the coal for several years. Poetic justice, I call it," said Oscar.

"Are you sure you aren't dreaming, too?" Coleen asked soothingly.

Oscar rolled over and dreamed about Maggie some more. After tossing and turning for hours during another erotic dream, he was shaken awake at 11 a.m. by a female hand. In a fog, he awoke and said, "Maggie, what were you saying about ... ?"

"I'm not Maggie," said Coleen angrily.

"Oh, mercy, she was in my dream. That's all. I'm sorry, Coleen. I was dreaming about her. Now I remember you were going to tell me what you knew about Manhattan," he said expectantly.

"Well, you'll just have to wait until next month until I get back from holidays in Kansas City."

"Aw, Coleen ... ," he started to say.

"I mean it. Next month," and she swept out of the room.

X

The day was August 7, and Oscar was pacing anxiously around the small airport waiting room at Whitehorse. He didn't know what the Canadian Pacific Airlines DC-3 from Edmington would bring.

He was sure it would bring Coleen back from a month-long holiday. She had gone away in a huff after what he considered a meaningless spat and he hadn't heard from her. Was this to be a catastrophe for him? Would she ever speak to him?

Then there were garbled reports from Japan of a bombing raid which had practically blown the City of Hiroshima off the map and thousands of people with it. Was this likewise a catastrophe the like of which the world had never before seen? Would the truth come out today from somewhere?

Coleen spotted Oscar when she came in the door. He spotted her, too: haggard and shaken with a haunted look in her eye. "Oh, my God, Oscar," she quavered, "now you know what my secret is all about. A terrible catastrophe hit the world yesterday. The pundits are saying the long-haired physicists have let nuclear physics get away from them and out of control with that bomb they let off over Hiroshima. They are saying in Edmington it is not an ordinary big bomb, but an atomic bomb made from fissionable material so that it can blow up the world and nobody will be safe any more."

"Is this the secret Manhattan Project you knew about?" he asked fiercely. "Is this the Manhattan Project I overheard those military people talking about on that trip over Canol No. 1 to Norman Wells? You tried to tell me Manhattan was in Chicago and I knew it was in New York. And when I contacted Cecil (The Bull) about it he treated me as if I was a bit looney-tunes."

"The rumors are — and I think they are true — that scientists working at the University of Chicago stadium for the U.S. Army developed that bomb with uranium oxide obtained in the Northwest Territories," she said. "The scientists obtained it from Eldorado Mining and Smelting which has that top-secret mine at Port Radium, a stone's throw from Norman Wells on Great Bear Lake. Yes, that was part of the Manhattan Project."

"Therefore you were right in your suspicion the reason the U.S. Army kept the Canol Project going after you figured it was a white elephant was to camouflage the Manhattan Project's source of raw ore," said Oscar in an awed tone.

She pulled him down on the bench beside her telling him the way she had seen things evolve from an insider's point of view. "What I discovered was that a group of British and French atomic scientists had been moved from Europe and North Africa to Montreal to try to achieve nuclear fission. Ore from the Eldorado mine was being allocated to them and the Americans at Chicago by the Canadian government. Some hard feelings had sprung up between the two groups over the allocation. The aggressive Americans thought the British-French group was dithering and didn't deserve the amount of uranium oxide being allocated to them. The U.S. Army directed both the Manhattan Project and the Canol Project. The Americans had a large number of soldiers on the Canol Project and kept them there so that if they weren't getting the amount of ore they wanted, they could despatch soldiers to the mine to take it. Who was to stop them? The Canadians had no military presence in the North."

"Now I see the picture. We in Canada were lucky we didn't get into a fight with the U.S. Army. That could have been tragic. You were onto a story, as we now see it, that is bigger than you and me. Had we succumbed to the temptation to leak that story in the face of the atomic bomb revelation yesterday, we might have been far out of our depth and charged with treason," Oscar sighed.

"Yes, we had a close call," Coleen agreed. "Now that the war is over and the U.S. is fending off criticism for using this terrible weapon against humanity and Canada finds itself complicit in supplying the raw material for the bomb, we will be able to tell the inside story." Rising and slipping her arm through his, she asked coyly, "Oscar, will you take me on a trip to Port Radium some time this year?"

"Definitely," he agreed. He felt as though he owned the town, with Coleen clutched tightly to him as if for protection from the suddenly big outside world.

A few days later he bought a Liberty Magazine and found in it a story by Dick Sanburn about the beginnings of the Manhattan Project. Contrary to popular belief, Manhattan was not created in panic and haste by a nation at war. It had its aegis in one of the most famous letters ever penned. The letter was written by Albert Einstein, who had become worshipped in the scientific community for his "theory of relativity," which practically nobody understood but everybody listened to. On August 2, 1939, his facile pen went to work on a letter to President Roosevelt of the United States warning him of the dangers of nuclear power.

"Look at what Sanburn quotes Einstein as telling Roosevelt," Oscar read out to Coleen. "He said recent work in France, Germany and the U.S. has made it possible to set up nuclear chain reaction in a large mass of uranium oxide. The phenomenon could lead to the construction of bombs. A single one carried by boat and exploded in a port might very well destroy the whole port."

The two main sources of supply then available to the U.S. were Canada and the Belgian Congo.

In view of this situation, Einstein suggested Roosevelt might form a linkage between his administration and the physicists working on chain reaction; that the U.S. government might search out uranium for the physicists and finance more research facilities.

The great scientist pointed out Germany was working on chain reaction and was replicating some of the U.S. work on uranium testing.

"Whadda ya know! His letter was written a year after Roosevelt had learned German scientists had been making progress on a bomb using Czechoslovakian uranium. It was also written two years before the president took us into war when the Japanese pulled that dastardly attack on Pearl Harbor," said Coleen. "By that time, American scientists were at work in earnest attempting to build an A-bomb small enough to be transported by air. Dick Sanburn is really good sourcing material from high authorities. Do you know him?"

"He was a great Canadian war correspondent who knows his way around. He contacted me once on a story he was writing about the Canol Project. His story in Liberty on how President Roosevelt followed up Einstein's suggestion is instructive. Listen to this:

"In 1938, by a strange coincidence, Otto Hahn and Fritz Strassman of Berlin had found that bombarding uranium oxide with neutrons produced barium. Barium is half the weight of the uranium. Implausibly, the two scientists couldn't figure out the importance of their discovery. Lise Meisner, a young Jewish colleague of Hahn, realized they had accidentally achieved fission, i.e., split a heavier nucleaus into lighter pieces. She cried 'Eureka' and took her theory out of Germany. Word of its importance evidently reached Roosevelt. Acting upon the importance of the discovery, Roosevelt was able to extract the huge sum of $2 billion from the U.S. Treasury to give the Manhattan Project the go-ahead at four secret locations. Manhattan's terms of reference were to make a self-sustaining nuclear reactor fissionable and compact enough to be used in a bomb."

Coleen added, "And since Brigadier General Brehon B. Somervell's job under the G-4 section of the U.S. Army was to requisition munitions, including components for an atomic bomb, the Manhattan Project came under his command, as well as the Canol Project."

"Now I'll tell you why Canada came into the picture on this great adventure," Oscar said. "The U.S. had one big hang-up. They had no good-quality uranium oxide. However, from his contacts in Canada, Somervell found that Gilbert LaBine's Eldorado Mining and Smelting had a small amount stockpiled at a refinery at Port Hope, Ontario, which had been abandoned. Initially, Somervell secured enough to fill the big squash court at the University of Chicago, one of the Manhattan Project secret locations. The scientists used graphite as a moderator and, glory be, this small amount achieved a self-sustaining chain reaction December 2, 1942."

The Chicago researchers came back to LaBine for more uranium. Although the supply at Port Hope had all been used up, he had had the intuition to reopen his abandoned mine at Port Radium. That was achieved under extreme secrecy. Like the Canol Project, the mine's existence wasn't officially admitted for a year after their start. The army required everyone going into that war zone, including the FBI, to sign an oath of secrecy.

"Yep, I had to sign that oath," Coleen admitted. "I heard some whispering around our office, but I had no idea what the boys were talking about. Neither did anyone tumble to the fact we could ever have become involved in the slightest way with the bomb development."

"Despite all precautions, you know, Canol secrecy was broken," continued Oscar. "It happened when Senator Richard Hamberger of Oregon came in here as an aide to General Patsy O'Connor. Of all things, he was also an accredited war correspondent for the Portland Bazoo. He wrote a story contending the Canol Project was a waste of taxpayers' dollars. When I saw this story I got in touch with Cecil (The Bull) and kidded him about it; that Hamberger was usurping the job of the FBI — and there were more wheels-within-wheels than I could figure out. Cecil became deathly quiet at this point and I knew something eerie was happening."

"I did hear Mr. Sverdrup once say that O'Connor was a bit upset at the Hamberger story. It sort of blew the cover on Canol's tight security. What bewildered me was why a senior officer didn't cashier a junior. I'm not sure if O'Connor knew about those ore shipments out of Port Radium. He never did figure out why the military was kept in the Canadian North so long."

"Maybe General O'Connor never had the nerve to call Senator Hamberger on the carpet the way General Somervell called Senator Harry Truman to heel. They called Somervell to testify at a subcommittee hearing aimed at finding out where all the money on Canol was going. Somervell had secrecy regulations on his side and his one-sentence reply to Truman was 'Senator, it will cost taxpayers less to keep Canol going than it will to abandon it at this point.' Truman didn't have a leg to stand on."

Truman didn't pursue the Canol issue. There were dozens more demanding issues in Washington and even more piled on him when President Roosevelt died in office. One of his first challenges a few months later when he was elevated to the presidency was what to do with the atomic bomb manufactured from Canadian uranium oxide.

"Sanburn claims Truman had doubts about using the bomb. However, he was dragged along by the Manhattan Project for which Roosevelt had provided the funds. Doubters were shoved aside. The bomb had devoured its prophets and there was no way he could then opt out of ordering it to be dropped. He was vindicated, though, when the war with the Japanese came to an abrupt end when the bomb was dropped," Oscar philosophized.

"Why did you use the word 'vindicated'? How could he vindicate a guilty conscience for attacking a civilian population?" Coleen asked.

"I don't think he was any more guilt-ridden than Gilbert LaBine, the man who single-handedly supplied the Americans with the product of his mine that made him an instant folk hero when it was used to instantly stop a war," replied Oscar.

"I don't quite follow you," said Coleen.

"OK. But you have to go back to the time the Manhattan Project came into the picture with bigger demands than LaBine could supply from the Port Hope stockpile. As I told you before, the Manhattan Project was competing with the British-French team in Montreal for product at Port Hope. Sanburn says it then became necessary for American-born C.D. Howe, Canadian minister of munitions and supply, to allocate the supplies on an equitable basis to the two groups. Prime Minister Mackenzie King, who had American leanings, had given Howe carte blanche for the man-killing task of equipping a fighting force of Canadians in Europe to help smash the German-Italian Axis. But crushed by a load of responsibility, Howe, in turn, delegated the task of allotting the Port Hope ore supply," Oscar related.

"How did this LaBine character fit into this scene?" asked Coleen.

"By default," answered Oscar.

"Isn't he the one who busted the Belgian radium cartel back in the 1930s?"

"One and the same. Now listen carefully and I'll tell you how LaBine became a real folk hero the first time. A brilliant Ontario prospector, he helped organize Eldorado to mine a claim of silver and pitchblende 10 years ago at Port Radium."

"I thought we were talking about radium. What's this pitchblende?" demanded Coleen.

"It's a heavy lustrous black mineral. It contains radium and uranium oxide. Got that straight? OK. Pitchblende ore contains radium in a ratio of 1 in 3 million. Radium was used in the early-day treatment of cancer. Because Port Hope was near the source of chemicals used to extract the radium, LaBine built the world's largest radium refinery there. Thus he was able to bust the Belgian cartel which was charging $50,000 an ounce for radium. Out of humanitarian considerations, he cut the price to $25,000. Got that straight also?" asked Oscar.

"What a man! Now I can see why he became a folk hero among the sick. Where did the uranium oxide disappear to?"

"It didn't, despite the fact it was a useless mineral which was used in coloring for ceramic tiles and flower pots, but sold for only $2.68 a pound. So it was stockpiled at Port Hope in big silos."

"Cripes," expostulated Coleen. "No wonder people got cancer with it around them in their homes."

"But nobody realized how dangerous exposure to it was then. When the war broke out, that was the end of LaBine's sale of radium and there was nothing to do but close the mine. The company controller, Kathie Bailie, was told to dispose of the assets. But she had a sixth sense about allowing the uranium oxide in the silos to be dispersed. She became the white-haired girl when the British and Americans came looking for uranium oxide at a much higher price than $2.68. But that supply was not enough. The United States military gave Howe money to have the mine pumped out in 1941 to start uranium oxide production again. The pump-out required six months."

"Two things I have to know," said Coleen. "Did any of the miners refuse to dig out this death-dealing mineral and whatever happened to that good silver ore that was dumped on the tailings pile? Didn't anyone think that was odd?"

"You women and your questions," growled Oscar. "I think some of the company officials suspected something was in the wind because the Manhattan Project opened up every aspect of need such as boats, barges, engine parts and labor. But nobody even knew the concept of atom bombs then. The operators of the concentrator plant were puzzled over the fact good silver ore was being discarded. Some of them had it in their head to come back and work the tailings pile on the sly at a future date."

"It must have pleased LaBine to take his mine out of mothballs and see it back in production," Coleen said. "I have another question for you and Sanburn. LaBine was a singular Canadian who became a folk hero for supplying the tools which have changed the course of warfare as it enabled enemies to make mass killings; and he also was a folk hero for helping to save the lives of cancer patients. I wonder how he lived a double life and kept sane?"

"Another leading question. However, I don't think LaBine had much time to do much agonizing over that moral question. He found himself in the centre of a tremendous uproar when it was discovered one of his over-zealous assistants contracted all uranium oxide from Eldorado to the Americans at Chicago. Officials managed to keep the lid on this inadvertently breached agreement due to wartime censorship and secrecy. It made Prime Minister Winston Churchill of Great Britain furious and he let Canada know he equated it as a body blow almost as severe as the British colony of Singapore falling to the Japanese. He railed mightily that for all intents and purposes the Yanks had a corner on the supply of ore. This was not the fault of Howe, but he got the blame. He was devastated that he had received a fierce blast from a suspicious Churchill about his ancestry and his loyalty. He was even accused of selling the British Empire down the river. Faced with a multiplicity of difficulties in his portfolio and then having his loyalty called into question by Churchill played havoc with his health."

Wartime secrecy cloaked the fact Howe was in such a fragile state of health that he nearly faltered. He was out on a golf course with his trusted friend and confidant, Dr. C.J. Mackenzie, president of the National Research Council, when he collapsed at the 11th hole. Aides rushed to him, prepared for the worst. Then he called for a drink of water. This brought him around and he soldiered on. Not even the astute Sanburn learned of the near-catastrophe at the time.

"Sanburn was astute enough to figure out that Howe needed a holiday, but he couldn't let down the side by taking time off. Things were in a mess. That was normal for Howe and others who were overburdened with war work: trying to be in so many places at one time and not having time to sit down to clarify things with their subordinates who were also overburdened," Oscar said. "In this case it was LaBine who could have told him the U.S. Army was more aggressive than anyone who was handling Canada's assets ever realized."

Coleen's view was that the U.S. atomic team was "the only one with a hope of developing the bomb in time to do any good. The Japanese had pulled out of the Aleutians and the U.S. Navy had broken the back of the Japanese fleet in the south Pacific, but they hung on resolutely. The Americans were desperate for a quick way to end the war without greater loss of life. I had heard mutterings around our office that the U.S. Army 'might have to step in' with a big surprise, but I had no idea what this meant. But it meant that the army might have had to step in and take over the Eldorado mine from Canada. That would have caused a real fuss and mess, wouldn't it? I am sure Howe knew the Americans were far ahead of the British-French team, but he somehow had to mollify that team. I presume Mackenzie knew that, too. And I presume that's the reason Howe gave Mackenzie the unenviable job of going to New York to the Manhattan Project headquarters to face Somervell to plead for release of ore which LaBine's assistant mistakenly gave the Americans. Mackenzie was promised enough to satisfy the British-French team."

"Coleen, you have analyzed this situation very well. But maybe you don't realize we have a faction in this country whose members have been shouting that you and your fellow Yankees have already 'invaded' the Northwest Territories, built airports without even telling the Canada Department of Transport and plan to grab all the Canadian scheduled airline routes to the Orient now that the war is over."

"Oh, you're talking about the Communists?" she asked brightly. "I've heard of a subversive by the name of Tim Buck who won a seat in the Canadian House of Commons."

"Can I quote you on all that?" Oscar responded. "If I said it I'd be shouted down by pinko bleeding hearts who are in the majority in Ottawa. These left-leaning 'politicos', as my friend, Maggie McMurphyvisk, calls them, cannot be convinced by the establishment, historians and nuclear scientists that the U.S. Army under President Roosevelt would ever resort to any bullying or undue pressure in the remotest sense; the Americans regard Canada too highly for that. But you must not overlook the fact that the U.S. Army had actually walked in and 'squatted' on Canadian soil during the construction of Northwest Territory airports serving the Canol Project. They also made extensive use of those airports for ferrying personnel in and out of Port Radium and for transporting uranium oxide via an emergency airlift."

"You have a big problem in Canada accommodating everyone," murmured Coleen.

"And I also know that the Yanks and Canucks have a pretty good tribunal for dealing with this kind of cross-border situation peacefully rather than with Sherman tanks. It is the Canada-U.S. Permanent Joint Board on Defence."

"Yes, I know of it."

"Did you ever know this board met and came to a startling conclusion the American military had pretty well run the Canadian North for a period of several months?"

"No, I didn't."

"The chief reason for this so-called invasion was the Department of Transport had no personnel on site to impress upon the American uniforms they were on Canadian soil without any deeds to the property which they were occupying. A couple of incidents made it onto the floor of the House of Commons. You know, like the time a desk-bound DOT bureaucrat from Ottawa was sent North to 'case' the situation. He got along famously with all those uniforms. But he became a damn nuisance so they kidnapped him and took him to the officers' mess at Camp Canol. After every complaint he made, the American brass hollered: 'Yes, we'll drink to that.' The DOT man demanded doubles. Next morning the officers poured him onto a plane bound for Ottawa with a note in his vest pocket: 'Ottawa declared war on Japan before Washington. Now we're all in this together.'"

Coleen roared with laughter. "How quaint. The point appears to be nobody knew better than Howe that, had the Americans chosen to make a move, Canada was in no position to do much about it."

"I couldn't agree more now that I have seen the facts," said Oscar.

Ottawa finally realized the problem was a shortage of DOT personnel in the North to put a short leash on pushy Yanks. A few DOT teams were dug out of cushy posts and ordered north. That ended the incipient War of the Northwest Territories.

"I'm astounded by your grasp of Canadian history," Coleen said admiringly. "Canadian history is full of stories that would have made front-page news in their time, but never got published. It's a sad situation here that Canadian publishers never gave as much ink to folk heroes as we do in the U.S. Canadians seem to be hero-challenged."

"Sadly, that happens all too frequently. Sanburn told me another startling piece of history which involved Mackenzie versus the British. Believe it or not, Mackenzie was forced to hotfoot it into the office of the British High Commissioner in Ottawa after he had learned the commissioner was about to make a call to Howe to instruct him not to make any more uranium oxide contracts with the U.S. Army. Mackenzie ordered the commissioner not to make that call to Howe or the War of the Northwest Territories might break out as Howe's answer would have been to go to hell and take his crowd of nuclear scientists back to Great Britain. In addition to keeping warring factions apart so the fighting forces would not be deprived of their weapons of war, Howe's job required him to maintain the secrecy of his supply chain. As the policy applied to the Manhattan Project, Howe expropriated Eldorado Mining and Smelting and its subsidiary, Northern Transportation, making them both Crown corporations. He felt that better security would be offered to Eldorado under government ownership and he assumed German spies and military intelligence couldn't breach the security. His method was to have the government quietly buy up Eldorado shares. He also didn't want the Germans to get wind of what was going on at Port Radium or learning about the fighting over the allocation of uranium oxide. The spy situation, which Howe guessed wrong, came as a shock to him as, while the Canadian and Russian armies were pummelling the German wehrmacht, the Russians were spying against us."

"Those obscene Commies," spat out Coleen. "I suppose Howe's office was filled with the bastards."

"No, the bastards compromised him more than that. One of the Russian spies was Dr. Allan Nunn May, a British scientist for the Montreal nuclear researchers for 10 years. Listen to what Dick Sanburn wrote about them:

"Not only was the Montreal group infested with spies from the Soviet Union, but the FBI lost a running battle to keep them out of the Manhattan Project. The Manhattan Project came near to being a nest of spies. It was rare for the U.S. Office of Strategic Services to keep anything hush-hush. The Kremlin probably knew more about the American war effort than President Roosevelt.

"You look a little surprised that Sanburn got away with publishing this. I think the reason he did was nobody would believe it," said Oscar.

"I also heard from Cecil (The Bull) that the Russian KGB spying was more extensive in the U.S. than Canada. The KGB was often able to double-check the results of atomic experiments at Los Alamos. And, in fact, it was suspected Joe Stalin knew of the bomb's existence long before Harry Truman was informed. What do you think of that?"

"Hey, this sounds like the comedy scripts of Jack Benny and Fred Allen I used to hear on the radio," bleated Coleen. "It's all so funny and entertaining I'm almost choked up. But I can only reiterate Somervell had to have some reason for keeping the Canol Project going."

"Do you believe Sanburn's contention that the Russians asked for seven tons of uranium oxide from Eldorado — but Howe turned them down? I think this stupidly brutal request by the Russians made Howe suspicious of a leak in the British atomic energy program. How's Howe to think of the British when he gets a shocker like that?" asked Oscar.

"But I heard Howe's real motive for favoring the Americans was the fact he had picked up a rumor Churchill had a spy in his cabinet," said Coleen.

"We sound like a couple of conspirators. Even so, our speculation is not so far from reality. Sanburn says the truth is that a spy by the name of John Cairncross gave Stalin the details of the British atomic weapons project as early as September, 1941," concluded Oscar. "Cairncross was secretary to Minister Without Portfolio Lord Hankey of Great Britain."

"Did you say Lord Haw Haw?"

Oscar laughed. "Who knows?"

The fact they treated this turn of events with levity somewhat shell-shocked Coleen. She had a glazed look in her eyes and sat there looking frightened and forlorn. Oscar gathered her up in his arms and held her and they stood together in silent contemplation of the events that had over-taken them, but were not aware of until after they happened.

"And what did you find out on your trip outside?" asked Oscar. "Did your folks believe the people and the adventures with which you had become entangled in the middle of Nowhere, Canada?"

"One thing you will be interested to know is that I am not pregnant."

Oscar stepped back with a sigh of relief. "Then I can tell you another secret. I've arranged with Bud Buckle to fly us into Port Radium the day after tomorrow. Be ready."

"I'm ready for anything," she teased, and she took off his shoes and pulled a new pair of socks onto his feet. "They're for all those nylons you brought me!"

On Thursday Buckle put his bush-pilot know-how to work to guide his Norseman to a dot on the eastern shore of Great Bear Lake. He landed and coasted into a host of hungry mosquitoes on the Eldorado dock. Here they could see the grey mine buildings from which a small group of Canadians and Inuit had unwittingly provided the wherewithal for the world's most historic and horrifying explosion.

Buckle, who had flown out some shipments of ore in the emergency airlift, showed them around the site he had come to know so well. Before he left them to walk hand-in-hand through the skimpy Arctic bush under which the mysterious pitchblende lay, he gave them a speech. "There is nothing much here to indicate that mankind has the power to dig this scarce ore lying 1,000 feet below our feet and smelt it into new products. One of them has been used for the consummate good of the people and the other the utmost evil. Nowhere but at Port Radium has pitchblende been formed underneath us into veins of ore in a manner which only geologists can explain. What I can't really fathom further is that when the fissionable material is smelted from the pitchblende it can kill thousands. But when under man's control, the same ore can create nuclear power for man's benefit."

They walked off to think over Buckle's profound exposition of a Northwest Territories mystery. They were still holding each other tightly when Buckle walked up behind them and tapped Oscar on the shoulder. "I can see that you two are not fissionable," he chuckled, "but it's time to go."

Coleen turned around and gave Buckle a big bear hug and a kiss. "I'm glad you brought us here," she said looking up into his dilated eyes. "But why has there never been a cairn or a statue or some other marker erected on this historic site?"

Buckle and Oscar were taken by surprise. They had never had to deal with a question like this before. Finally Buckle said: "To the uninitiated, this whole property is nothing but an unprepossessing hole in the ground in a hinterland most people will never get to see. Maybe it is best forgotten and unmarked."

"But there is nothing here to tell the world that Canada played a major part in supplying the ore which caused a terrible tragedy, yet provided a warning to the nations of the world they had finally reached the ultimate in wreaking their own destruction and it is time to quit," said Oscar.

"Yes," replied Buckle, "maybe this spot should be put on tourist maps. Maybe thousands will be interested in flying in here. This is a place where people may be able to come to solve the mystery of why we still arm people for war when there is now so much danger in doing that."

The trio walked away from this spectral enigmatic speck of real estate in the Northwest Territories silently engrossed in thoughts that had never been articulated before.

The rough flight back bounced Oscar out of his guilt-ridden reverie about the bomb into the reality that the bomb had blown him and Coleen out of jobs.

In Whitehorse, there was a message telling him to call Cecil (The Bull). Cecil was a bit sad, too. "Your orders are to come to Washington for debriefing by the FBI, and bring Coleen with you. Also, Senator Frank Jacobs wants you to have a visit with him. He may have a surprise for you."

Coleen also had an invitation. "Dad and Mom have asked me to come to St. Louis — and bring my young man with me."

"Wow," was all Oscar could think of to say.

He and Coleen survived the debriefing. On the way out Oscar was waylaid by his friend, Hughie Melvin, the FBI agent from Seattle who had hired him in Picture Butte and who had been promoted to Washington. After pleasantries had been exchanged, Melvin produced an envelope and said: "One thing we forgot. Here is a cheque for $10,000. It's for isolation pay." He grinned at Coleen. She got the message and walked up to Melvin and kissed him on the lips.

She was ready the next day with another big buss for Senator Jacobs. "Perhaps you two would like to appear in the visitors' gallery of the Senate this afternoon and be recognized," he said, and then added: "Everyone's assignment turned out very much different than any of us ever expected."

They took off for St. Louis and made a side trip to Reno, Nevada, where Coleen taught Oscar enough to win $15,000 at the tables.

As a result of their visit to Reno, a few weeks later Mr. and Mrs. Oscar Grove walked into the Picture Butte Bugle newsroom. It was much the same as Oscar had left it four years ago, except that Peck Barnard had become a tired, overworked old man. He was a bit jaded because he wanted to retired, but couldn't find a decent successor. After trading industry gossip for a while, he asked, "What do you plan to do in this business with all that experience you have under your belt, Oscar?"

"The first requirement is to find a job where I can make some money."

"Is that so? Well, let's adjourn to the back booth of the T-Bone Restaurant, chase away the flies and see what we can do about that."

After a couple of drinks, Peck relaxed, sat back and sighed once again: "How can I retire and let one of those cubs take over my job? What would you think about a job like this?"

Oscar looked at Coleen and saw an OK signal in her eye, which told him to sign up for the job.

"Tell me, Oscar, what would your first editorial sound like?"

"I'm glad you asked. I've been working on it for a few days. It will go something like this: *I'd like to introduce my readers to a new Canada. It is a new Canada which I discovered on a wartime assignment in the Northwest Territories. It is a Canada with which the readers may have trouble coping.*

"*Canada went into this war as a British colony at the behest of the Mother Country for whom we willingly provided cannon-fodder to fight another of her interminable world wars. Each war was to end all wars. But the Second World War finally did the trick, thanks to the atomic bomb. At the end of the war Canada freed itself from colonial ties and is started on the road to dictatorship.*

"*I saw what started out to be a simple defensive mechanism, that is, to build a highway (which we had been trying to get for 40 years) from Dawson Creek to Fairbanks and which ended up on the outskirts of a nuclear war.*

"*From my vantage point in the Northwest Territories I saw a warless world emerge; but the price was to become involved in intrigue, spying, malfeasance, the wasting of young lives and betrayal by our friendly nations. We were dragged into a world of great international events which shook the world, the biggest of which originated in Canada: the bomb. We trusted the Russians to help us win the war, but in doing so we may have lost the peace. The top-secret nuclear project was riddled with spies.*

"*American taxpayers paid heavily for an exercise in futility. The maddening part of it was the critics were right. The Canol Project should have been shut down before a mile of pipe was laid. A general, who depended on his right to make government policy a secret, hornswoggled his country's taxpayers. Oh, the futility. Oh, the waste. Oh, hell.*"

Lighting up a Tuero cigar, Peck looked through the smoke at Coleen and said, "Do you think this young man will make a good editor?"

Nothing could have surprised him more than Coleen's answer: "No, I don't think this young man will make a good editor. I think I will make a good editor. This young man and I have a $25,000 down payment to buy this paper. And Oscar will be the publisher."

"Well, Jeez ... why I never ... by God, you're a genius, young lady ..."

Coleen took both of Peck's hands: "Mr. Barnard, if Oscar can learn to drink as much overproof rum as you, he will make a good publisher. But let me add this to the libretto: You both must remember the United States of America came in and won a war which defeated two nations which had evil designs on our way of life. You helped in this struggle, too, because you had confidence in Oscar. Now it is time for you to quit agonizing, preaching, carrying a load of hair-shirt guilt, never smoke another one of those damn cigars and retire in comfort and dignity."

Peck looked at her and said, "Yes, it is time for me to write '---30---'. She hugged him.

Epilogue

During their trip to the Eldorado mine site with pilot Bud Buckle, Coleen raised the question about why a cairn, statue or other marker had never been erected on this spectral enigmatic speck in the Northwest Territories. The mine with its lode of uranium oxide provided a tacit warning to the nations of the world they had finally reached the ultimate in wreaking their own destruction and it is time to quit.

Not all Canadians agreed with her philosophical point of view. They became historical revisionists by bulldozing the mine site flat. All is silent in the bush again, as if nothing significant had ever happened at Port Radium, Northwest Territories.